VERBUM FORTIUS EST QUAM PECCATUM
CUM CULPA DIMIDIATA

STORY SYNOPSIS

At the end of book one of Mike Oliveri's werewolf noir series, *Winter Kill*, FBI special agent Angela Wallace lay in a hospital bed attempting to make sense of the bloody shootout with drug smugglers that nearly left her dead in the northern mountain range of Minnesota, and the mysterious, reclusive Tyler family that seems to be at the heart of all her questions.

Lie with the Dead continues Agent Wallace's search for answers, where the trail leads her to a deserted mining town in Nevada and, once again, finds herself fighting for her life against unseen enemies hell-bent on keeping dark secrets buried. But the truth she uncovers is deadlier than she ever imagined.

LIE WITH THE DEAD

ALSO BY MIKE OLIVERI

Winter Kill
Book One of *The Pack* Werewolf Noir Series

4x4
Collection, with Brian Keene, Geoff Cooper & Michael T. Huyck, Jr.

Deadliest Of The Species
Winner of the Bram Stoker Award for First Novel

To Travel Among Men
From *New Dark Voices*

Warning Signs
From *Brimstone Turnpike*

Werewolves: Call Of The Wild
Comic Book Limited Series

BOOK TWO

The Pack
LIE WITH THE DEAD

······································

MIKE OLIVERI

AN EVILEYE BOOK
March 2014

Published by
Pulp+Pixel Entertainment Company
301 E. Congress Parkway, #1981, Crystal Lake, IL 60039

Editorial Director: A.N. Ommus

Cover photo illustration, title and book design by Viktor Färro

Body background image: Shutterstock.com

The Pack and *The Pack: Lie with the Dead* logos
are trademarks of Pulp+Pixel Entertainment Company

ISBN: 978-0-9848800-5-8

For more information about this series or other books published by
Evileye Books, please visit Evileyebooks.com

Printed in the United States of America.

— 6:23 —

This one's for Brian, Mikey, Coop, and John.
There's a lot of road ahead of us yet, brothers.
We ride.

ACKNOWLEDGMENTS

Oh, the things these keys have seen since *Winter Kill*. I owe a huge thanks to a lot of folks for helping see this thing through, especially to my wife Melissa and The Rugrats for helping me stay sane.

Thanks to the gang at Time Flies for the good times, and to our friend, John Jameson, for speeding things along. Thanks to Steve H. for the motorcycle shows, and to Mark C. for the cigars. Thanks to my instructors at the AOK for kicking ass, and for teaching me to do the same.

I'd like to thank the good folks at Evileye Books for the keen editorial eyes, and for the patience. Thanks also to Cullen Bunn for the brainstorming and scheming (we'll get there, man). Thanks to Jason T. for having faith, and to all the *Pack* fans out there who came back for more. You all rock. \m/

LIE WITH THE DEAD

ONE

A GLIMMER IN THE DUSTY ROAD AHEAD caught Angie's eye, but by the time she recognized the spike strip, it was too late. Her front tires hissed and popped. Angie seized the wheel with both hands as the rear tires blew. Her foot hovered over the brake as the steering went spongy. The rented Malibu shuddered and lurched on its rims, spraying gravel into the wheel wells and kicking clouds of dust up in a whirlwind trail. Someone wanted her stopped. All the better in the middle of desert wasteland where bodies are nothing more than fertilizer.

She goosed the gas instead. The left front tire unraveled and flogged the quarter panel. The car slid off the main strip onto the pothole-pocked shoulder. The fender missed the corner of the faded and rotted "Welcome to Charity" sign by inches. The wheel rammed against the edges of the potholes. The impacts threw Angie forward and the seatbelt caught her hip, setting off an explosion of pain rivaling the bullet that shattered her hip in the snowy fields of the Tyler Lodge grounds six months back. She bit back screams as every little bump in the crumbling asphalt jolted her back and ass. She fought the urge to slam on the brakes as she steered back onto the desert road and barreled down Main Street into the abandoned town.

A thunderclap erupted off her left shoulder. The rear passenger window exploded. Tiny chunks of glass sprayed across the back seat. Something bit her just below the right ear. Two more shots came in rapid succession, and the rear window shattered and fell.

Angie kept her head down. The shooter had to be in one of the boarded-up storefronts she just passed. She swerved left as she approached the next intersection, then spun the wheel around to the right. The Malibu leaned into the turn, and the front left rim collapsed. The chassis bounced hard and ground across the asphalt. She jammed on the brakes, then threw off her seatbelt as the car shuddered to a halt. Her hand went straight to the .40-caliber SIG behind her hip as she pushed through the door and out of the car. Ducking low, she moved around the door and crouched behind the engine block. She extended the pistol over the hood in a two-handed grip, and scanned the right side of the street.

She expected Old West. Instead, Main Street Charity looked more Mayberry meets Omega Man. It looked like a quaint old place where kids would frequent soda shops and greasers would race muscle cars up and down the strip, until one day they all just up and left, abandoning it all to the desert winds.

A man stepped out of a doorway three doors down, one hand shielding his eyes from the sun, the other holding a long, black shotgun.

Angie sighted the man's center of mass. "Federal Agent! Drop the gun!"

The man froze. Angie recognized the panicked look, the tension of his body as he raised the weapon. She fired three quick shots and dropped him.

A bullet zipped past her head and the whipcrack of a rifle shot echoed down the street. She ducked down beside the wheel. The tang of melted rubber stung her nostrils. A second shot, then a third thudded into the hood.

"Ahh, shit . . ." The first shooter's shotgun rattled and clacked against the street. Angie looked beneath the car to spot him, but the lowered chassis, due to the flattened tires, made it difficult to see more than a few feet beyond the passenger side.

"You alright?" someone shouted. Another male, this one with a deep, booming voice. Probably the sniper.

"I'm fine!" the first shooter responded. "She hit my vest."

"How about you, lady? You drop your gun, poke that pretty little head out, maybe I won't blow it off!"

Pretty little head indeed. It went one of two ways with the bad guys: they either see the dark red hair and green eyes and think they can charm her out of her pants, or they see a slender woman just shy of five seven and think they can take her down easy. She enjoyed proving them wrong.

"Come on now," Sniper shouted. "Let's do this the easy way so no one gets hurt!"

His voice echoed down the street, making it difficult to pinpoint Shotgun's footsteps. He crossed to her side of the street, but she couldn't be sure how far away. Her bullets would slow him down some, even with the vest, but if he got close enough with that shotgun, he didn't need to be at the top of his game.

Angie crawled to the front of the car and peeked around the front bumper. Shotgun slipped into a recessed doorway two doors down. The whipcrack of the rifle echoed down the street again, and the bullet whacked the sidewalk two feet from the car's nose. Angie ducked back again, and a second bullet struck the sidewalk just a few yards ahead of the first. He had to be on the left side of the street, probably on the second floor.

"Last chance, lady!" Sniper shouted. "Next one doesn't miss!"

Hurried footsteps came closer, then shuffled aside. Shotgun was moving in. She couldn't stay here. Sniper would just keep her pinned down until Shotgun had a clear shot. The jewelry store in front of her had a recessed doorway, and the glass had been broken out of the door, but it was directly across from the passenger side and she didn't like the idea of having to run toward her shooters to get there. Running farther down the street guaranteed a bullet in the back, so she eyeballed the corner of the jewelry store.

If there were more gunmen coming to flank her from around that corner, it would be real trouble.

She didn't see any other option. She got off her knees and onto her toes, settling into a sprinter's starting position. Her hip burned from the tension. Footsteps approached, then another shuffle as Shotgun moved into the jewelry store's doorway.

Angie lunged forward, leading with her pistol. Shotgun started to bring up his weapon, then ducked back as she pulled the trigger. Her shot went wide, but it had the desired effect of backing him off. She sprinted around the corner and kept running across the street toward the back of the next building. The rifle barked behind her, but she was well out of sight now.

She leapt onto the next curb, stopped and spun. She swept her pistol across the narrow road behind the buildings and, seeing no signs of movement, shifted her aim to the corner of the jewelry store.

Shotgun peeked around the corner.

She put two rounds into the brick beside him. He ducked back for cover, giving her a chance to sprint behind the next building.

The street came off at a diagonal from the main street, passing a triangular lot with a rickety jungle gym and a crooked merry-go-round behind the jewelry store. The street continued past the abandoned gas station across from her. An alley stretched out in front of her for another block, with the backs of the Main Street stores on her left and the backyards of some homes on her right. A battered chain-link fence surrounded the gravel lot behind the service station, enclosing only the decaying hulks of three ancient cars and a stripped pickup.

She knew she had to get out of the alley quick. Sniper might be about to pop out a back door, or he might be regrouping with Shotgun so they could track her together. If they were smart—and she had to assume they were to set up an ambush—they'd have one man down Main Street and one covering the alley. They'd have the luxury of flushing her out one way or the other, or just sitting tight and waiting for backup. If she followed her first instinct and went into one of the buildings, it put her in their waiting game.

She sprinted across the alley and past the service station's lot, then ducked alongside the fence as she ran toward the back of the building. Her hip tightened up and burned, but she endured and darted across the yard between the service station and the first house. Her hiking boots crunched in the gravel drive, then she was up on the porch with her back to the wall.

Breathe, she told herself. She took a deep, steady breath through her nose, and released it through her mouth in an effort to get her heart rate under control. She stretched her right leg, and the pain in her hip faded from a sharp twinge to a dull throb. There was no sound of pursuit, but she dared not peek around the corner and risk giving away her new position. Instead, she stepped off the porch and crossed the street, moving kitty-corner to the next house and on to the backyard.

She moved through the backyards for cover. The desert had long ago reclaimed the ground, returning lawns to dust and desert flora. The remains of a wind chime clinked softly in the breeze, and though she'd likely be the first human being to have heard it in decades, she half expected children to erupt from a nearby door at any moment, or their fathers to come out to investigate the strange woman creeping through their yards.

Most of the homes were identical: small, blocky bungalows cut from the same mold and slapped together in a hurry, no doubt to support the burgeoning silver mine before it went bust. The desert scoured some of them of color, but even in the remainder Angie saw little variety. This one had a concrete stoop, that one a deck, a carport over there. Enough to give a home a hint of personality, but in the end they were all the same prefab crap dropped in a dead and crumbling pop-up town.

Angie chose the home with the collapsed picket fence, thinking maybe, just maybe, it would be enough of an obstacle that her assailants would assume she skipped it. She stepped over the downed rail, and winced as the planks and old nails creaked beneath her weight. Up two steps and across a porch just large enough for a chair and a cigar got her to the back door. The handle twisted back and forth with ease, but the mechanism didn't seem to engage. She turned the handle all the way to the right, braced her shoulder against the door, and pushed.

The wood barked softly as the door popped free of the jamb, then scraped across the tiled floor on the other side. She looked back and forth down the yards one more time, then slipped inside and, with gentle pressure, shoved the door back into the jamb. It didn't close all the way, but made a snug enough fit that someone passing from afar would see no sign of her entry.

Angie allowed herself to relax and limped deeper into the house. There was an old kitchen on her left, stripped of its appliances. A bedroom, a bathroom, and a living room. Her every step kicked up a small cloud of dust, and old webs hung from the corners. It smelled dry and stale, and she swallowed against a tickle in her throat.

Thin, moth-eaten curtains still hung from the front window, one side still secured by its tieback. She stayed a few paces back from it, but close enough she could see the street. She shifted her pistol to her left hand and massaged the front of her hip with her right.

Now that she had at least a few minutes of safety, she reached into her jacket pocket for her cell phone.

The cell phone still connected to the Malibu's cigarette lighter to keep it charged while she used the GPS.

She bit back a curse and kicked up a cloud of dust.

She checked her watch. The sun would set in another hour or so.

Stranded in a ghost town. Hunted by snipers. No way out. Her physical therapist—and the Bureau, for that matter—expected her to be kicking back on a San Diego beach for the next five days.

Fuuuck, me, she thought. It's going to be a long night.

TWO

"DAMN IT, WOMAN, will you get your big ass outta the way of the TV?" Tommy said.

Crystal turned and glared at him. "It's a frickin' commercial, asswipe."

"So what? Maybe I wanna buy a new truck!"

"That'll be the day." She reached above the television and pulled a mixing bowl out of the cabinet. Two smaller bowls tumbled out of it and bounced across the floor. "Those trucks probably cost more than this whole trailer. And I wouldn't have to walk in front of the TV if all these damn boxes weren't in the way!"

"Hey, this is important stuff! The cops would have just taken it all out of Mitch's place and burned it! What else am I supposed to do with it?"

"Oh, I don't know, how about hand the pamphlets out? They don't do any good sitting in boxes, lazy-ass!"

"Shut up, the show's coming back on."

She mumbled something more as she went back into the kitchen, but he drowned her out with the remote. Cranking up the volume would have to do until someone invented a way to mute her harpy ass.

Tommy was no dummy. He knew the money wasn't coming in, but he didn't have Mitch's connections. He was always content to be a soldier. Make a few drops, kick in a few teeth, get paid, worry about the rest later. It wasn't his fault Mitch got himself killed.

Tommy grabbed his bowl and his lighter off the lamp table and sparked up. He breathed in deep, and let it out slow.

"You best save some of that for me!" Crystal snapped.

"Shut the fuck up, I'm thinkin'."

"Yeah, well, don't strain nothin'."

Tommy believed in the Aryan cause. He really did. It was a lot easier to follow than lead, though. Slinging a little meth made ends meet, but it wasn't a fraction of the cash they brought in a few months ago. Mitch and Duff, they made shit happen. They had ideas. Plans. Goals.

Maybe he should have paid a little more attention, shown a little more ambition.

He took another long hit off the bowl. The other guys, they expected more out of him. He could see them drifting away, losing faith. The whispers, the sidelong glances, the sarcastic remarks . . . it all pointed to the end.

Crystal was no different. Used to be they'd party most every night. Now she was always working, always tired, always bitching about how he was smoking her weed. Just because she picked it up and brought it home, suddenly she can't share.

Fuck it. One more hit for inspiration. He held the smoke as he set the bowl and lighter aside again.

He needed to earn again. Bring in that cash, he'd have her respect again. Get out of this trailer and into a proper place. Bury her in bling. Or maybe just bury her. Either way, he'd be back to partying in no time. He leaned over and snatched a pamphlet out of the box, let his bleary eyes wander over the swastika on the cover.

Maybe Crystal had something there. A rally, that's what they needed. Spread the word, recruit some troops. Build up his own little army, just like Mitch put together. Find his own soldiers and expand his territory.

Yeah.

Oil sizzled in the pan in the kitchen. The aromas of chicken and spices filled the trailer. Tommy's stomach rumbled.

First he had to eat. Yeah. Tomorrow he could get started on the planning. Hopefully, she'll make mac 'n' cheese and mashed potatoes with the chicken. Oh, and gravy! Mmm, biscuits, too. His mouth watered.

Tump! Tump! Tump!

"Answer the door, would ya'?"

Crystal threw a spatula on the counter and went to the door. Yeah, he wasn't but eight feet from it himself, but the actress on this dancing show looked mighty fine in that tight, red dress. God bless high definition.

No shadow fell on the narrow, pebbled window mounted in the door. Crystal tried to peek out the window, but they had too much shit stacked in front of it, and condensation on the interior clouded her vision. She wiped some of it away with her fingers, but it didn't help much, just offering a smeared view of the yard. Someone stood at the bottom of the front steps, but she couldn't tell who. He climbed up again as she watched and reached for the door.

Tump! Tump! Tump!

"Quit fuckin' around and open the door already!" Tommy said.

"You expecting anyone?"

He shrugged. "Neighbor's pipes probably froze again. Tell him he shoulda kept his faucet on a trickle. I ain't goin' anywhere."

That couldn't be it, Crystal thought. It wasn't that cold anymore. She released the latch. The exterior door and the interior screen door shared a common hinge and swung outward together. She opened them halfway and leaned to see around the edge.

The visitor ripped the door out of her hand. She grasped the doorframe as she stumbled out, then the visitor punched her in the chest, dead center below her sternum. The blow knocked the wind out of her, but stopped her fall, and she stumbled back into the trailer, unable to draw another breath. Searing pain erupted from behind her breastbone. She dropped to her knees.

The visitor stepped into the room and slammed the door shut behind him.

"Hey, man! You can't . . ." Tommy let the words die as he got a good look at the visitor, at his black hoodie and the black bandana over his mouth and nose.

At the bloody knife in his hand.

Tommy had a gun. He knew he did. Where the fuck was it? He pawed at the lamp table, knocking his pipe and lighter and a half-empty can of Bud on the floor.

Crystal gulped for air, finally drawing a few shuddering breaths. Her hand, pressed to her stomach, felt warm and sticky. She looked down, saw the blood covering her palm and drenching the belly of her khaki t-shirt. She let out a weak croak of a scream, drew in another ragged breath.

Tommy flipped the table. The bulb in the lamp exploded, casting the end of the living room in shadow and white flickering light from the television. Where the fuck was that gun?

Crystal got out a full scream at last. The visitor grabbed her hair and yanked her head back. His blade sliced across her throat before she could get her hands up. Her scream cut to a gurgle. She clutched at her neck with both hands, tucking her chin in a vain attempt to contain the blood.

Behind the chair! Tommy remembered. He spun the chair to the left and reached back. His hand struck the shotgun's barrel propped against the window behind him. It rolled around the lip of the frame, scraped across the wall, and hit the floor with a clatter. Tommy spun the other direction and watched as the visitor stomp-kicked the center of Crystal's back. Her head snapped back as she fell forward, revealing the gaping wound across her neck. The visitor stepped over her legs and into the living room.

Tommy knew he couldn't beat the guy to the shotgun. He pushed out of his chair and circled toward the television. His hand found the folding knife in his front pocket. He pulled it out, shoved the small knob at the base of the blade with his thumb. The spring assist took over, and the blade flashed open with a solid click.

The visitor's narrowed eyes betrayed the smile behind the bandana over his face. He settled into a fighting stance, the knife low in his right hand, his left up in a guard position.

Tommy licked his lips. His knife was longer than the visitor's. Heavier. He could do this. He took a tentative step forward. The visitor didn't react. He jabbed a low feint, then raised his knife high for a downward slash.

The visitor stepped inside his reach and put up his left arm to catch Tommy's wrist on his forearm. A quick twist and he had Tommy's wrist locked up in an iron grip. His knife flicked once across the inside of Tommy's forearm, then twice across his body.

Tommy hissed with each cut and jumped back. His heel struck a box, and he almost went over backward. He couldn't feel his knife in his grip any more, and a squashed X across his chest oozed blood.

"Try again." The visitor pointed to the floor.

Tommy looked down at his own knife lying near his foot. He could barely close the fingers of his right hand. He crouched down and picked up the knife with his left hand, keeping his eye on the visitor the whole time. He rose and matched the visitor's stance.

"Who the fuck are you?" Tommy asked.

"The man putting you out of business."

"Do you know who I am? Who my friends are? They'll never stop looking for you!"

"I'm shakin'."

Tommy lunged forward, leading with the knife. The visitor twisted to one side and made a quick downward slash across Tommy's left wrist. Tommy yelped, then grunted as the visitor's left elbow caught him on the bridge of the nose. Tears filled his eyes and stars exploded across his vision. The visitor spun him around. One, two, three jabs to his kidney lit up his back with pain. One more stab between the ribs for good measure, and the visitor shoved him away.

He collapsed to his knees and propped himself up on his chair. He couldn't draw the breath to scream. It felt like someone parked a car on his chest. His side and back burned. Hot blood cascaded down the back of his leg. Black closed in around the edges of his vision as he craned his neck to see the intruder crouching down beside him.

"This is Sword territory now," the man said.

Tommy blinked. He couldn't muster the strength to move. The knife slipped from his fingers, hit the floor with a soft thump. The pain faded and grew distant.

His last breath hitched in his throat.

THREE

THE OLD DIESEL PICKUP RUMBLED through the
desert at better than seventy miles an hour. Its high-
beams slashed the darkness, yet barely picked out the old
road surface beneath the sand and dirt. It didn't seem to
bother Sheriff Jerome Hess as he steered the truck
through the occasional curves with ease. He marked off
the miles with measured puffs of the cigar clenched
between his teeth. The smoke filled the cabin and
threatened to choke out his passenger, Cole Tyler, riding
shotgun.

The cigar stank of stale earth and faded leather, a scent
Cole would forever associate with the old bastard next to
him. Middle age had softened the sheriff's muscles, but
he more than made up for it with a hardened tempter.
His stout paunch and soft features gave him a jolly,
affable look, but anyone he pulled over would soon find

that wasn't the case. The two years since Cole last saw the man did little to take the edge off, and added a few more wrinkles to his weathered hide. The pepper had shaken loose from his hair, leaving only dingy gray and dirty white.

Jesus, Cole thought. Two years already? He wondered how different things would be—if he would be sitting here right now—had he blown the sheriff's brains out that night. Marcus Rice may have been responsible for the death of Cole's brother, Will, but Hess had pulled the trigger. Letting Hess live was the smart play, but deep down Cole often questioned whether it was the right play.

Cole opened his window six inches, letting the dense smoke out and the cool air in. The landscape looked as barren and dead as the snow-covered wilderness back home. At least the landscape back home would be coming back to life in the next few weeks.

He stifled a yawn. A sleepless night and an early flight left him drained. If he hadn't taken the time to down a few sandwiches before Hess picked him up at the motel, he'd really be in bad shape.

"It wasn't a call for help, you know." Hess rolled down his window and tossed out the stub of his cigar. "My men and I can handle this."

"I know," Cole said. "This isn't about trust. It's personal."

"Fair enough. I just called because . . . well, because I owe you. That's all."

Damn right he did. Cole suspected that was as close as Hess would come to offering an apology.

"Marcus Rice was a lot of things, but to kill his own brother and frame yours? Ain't nobody saw that comin'. Charlie Rice was a damn good man, not a thing like Marcus."

Shit. The only thing worse than a half-assed apology? An explanation. Cole rubbed his nose to hide his scowl.

"When I found Charlie all tore up in his own home like that . . . I guess it tore me up some, too. I let it get personal, and Marcus's explanation was the easy one."

And there it was. But it didn't explain why Kate had to die, too. Why Cole and his mother had to cook up a bullshit story for her father, and accept responsibility for her death because she eloped with Will.

"I have to wonder, sheriff, how many other innocents you've got buried out in this desert."

"Because of Marcus?"

"Because you were all tore up over something."

Hess chuckled. "Fair enough. Let's just say you're the first to come looking for any of 'em."

Silence fell between them for the next mile.

"Listen," Hess said then, "I've been meaning to ask you somethin'. Ever since Marcus bit me, I've been having some nasty dreams. If you bite someone, does it, you know, change them?"

"No."

"You sure? I mean, how did you become . . . the way you are?"

"I was born this way," Cole said. "Same as my brother, and same, I imagine, as the Rice brothers."

"Huh."

"Do you have any idea whether Charlie Rice had any native blood in him?"

"Yeah. A couple generations back, I think. I take it you're full blood?"

"Yeah."

"Never did take you for an Irishman."

Cole laughed.

"Why, does Indian blood have something to do with it?" Hess asked.

"I have no idea." It wasn't a lie. Mom didn't have a lot of answers, and he never got the chance to ask his father.

"Huh," Hess said again. "As it happens, Charlie Rice was full of surprises. But we're here. We can talk more about that later."

Wonderful, Cole thought.

Hess tapped the brakes. They rode past the crumbled remains of a wooden sign and the headlights fell on the sides of a pair of brick buildings flanking the road. The street and buildings alike were dark. Hess turned off the high beams.

"We're here."

"Where's 'here'?"

"Charity. It's another old mining town."

"Where is everyone?"

"About fifty years back, the mining company went chasing a bad seam. The explosion triggered a sinkhole on the north side of town, which swallowed half a block and killed a couple dozen people. Two days later, three more people died and they figured out they screwed up the well, too. Between the unsteady ground and the poisoned water, the people couldn't leave fast enough."

"So you had Wallace sent out here for a nice, private chat?"

A man in desert camouflage walked out into the path of the headlights. He held a shotgun in his right hand, the butt resting under his ribs and the barrel pointed skyward. He waved down the pickup with his other hand.

"We're about to find out." Hess stopped the pickup a few feet short of the man, and killed the engine. He left the headlights on as he climbed out.

Cole got out on the other side. He sized up the man with the shotgun. The guy was tall, maybe six inches taller than the sheriff. Dark red hair peeked out from beneath his khaki baseball cap, and a red beard filled out his jaw. His arms and face were lean, and Cole realized the padding he'd first taken as muscle was a bulletproof vest.

There were two neat holes in the man's shirt, right over his left pectoral muscle.

"What have we got, Harv?" Hess asked him.

"There's a problem, Boss. We've lost her somewhere in town."

"Goddamn it. This was supposed to be a simple job!"

"I know, but she was armed!"

"Of course she was armed," Cole said. "She's a federal agent."

Hess and his man exchanged a glance.

"And why the fuck didn't you tell me this on the phone last night?"

"You mean she didn't identify herself that way?" Cole asked.

"Hell no. We'd be handling this a lot differently if we knew she was a goddamn fed!"

Strange, Cole thought. She should have announced herself to the sheriff when she first arrived. What was she up to?

"Where is she now?"

"We're not sure," Harvey said. "But she's not going anywhere! Check it out." He reached into the large cargo pocket on the side of his thigh and pulled out a chunky cell phone and a key ring with a key, a black plastic fob, and a white rental tag on it.

Cole looked over at the car sitting at the end of the block, not quite past the reach of Hess's headlights. He noticed both tires on the passenger side had blown out, and the front end had ground onto the sidewalk.

Hess took the phone and keys and stuffed them in the pocket of his vest. "You still haven't answered my question."

"We didn't expect her to shoot back. I tried to put a scare into her with the shotgun, and she put me on my ass." He touched a finger to one of the bullet holes in his shirt. "Then she ran off down a side street and we lost her."

"What have you been doing since? Where the hell is Sam?"

"We looked for her, but when it started getting dark we stashed the Jeep and took watch on her car. Sam's up on the roof."

"How far's the nearest town?" Cole asked.

"Sunset's twenty-two miles back," Hess said. "That's it."

"Then she isn't going anywhere."

"How do you know that?"

"Because she's got a bad hip."

"Yeah, she left a cane in the car, too," Harvey said.

Hess spat a thick glob of phlegm on the street. "Just how well do you know this woman, Tyler?"

Cole shrugged. "There was an incident back home last fall, and she took a bullet. I haven't talked to her since, but I doubt she's in any shape to run a marathon."

"Well, we have no choice now." Hess drew his pistol from his hip holster and checked the chamber, then returned it to his hip. "We need to find her and finish the job."

"Not before I talk to her," Cole said. "You know I can find her, but I need to know what she's doing here and what she knows."

He felt some relief the Bureau may not have sent her. That didn't mean they wouldn't come looking for her if she disappeared, though. And if the Bureau didn't send her down on a lead, then what was her angle?

Hess took off his cowboy hat and smoothed his hair. He fiddled with the brim of the hat for a moment. "It's gonna be a lot harder to take her alive, assuming we even find her."

"She's in the middle of the desert with no food or water. She's got to come out sometime."

"Alright, here's how we'll play it. I'm going to call in a few more guys. We'll spread out, flush her out. We catch her, you get first crack at her. But if she doesn't come quietly and catches a bullet . . ." Hess shrugged. "Shit happens."

"All I ask is we try."

"Then I guess I've got some calls to make." Hess put his hat back on and returned to the truck.

Cole extended a hand to the man with the shotgun. "Cole Tyler."

"Jim Harvey." He took Cole's hand in a firm grip, pumped it once.

"Are you a deputy?"

"Yep. You're the guy who took down Marcus Rice?"

"That's right."

Harvey nodded. "Son of a bitch had it coming. Charlie was good people. Any man who kills his own kin deserves to be put down."

He grunted a vague affirmative. "I'm going to go check out the car."

Harvey made a go-ahead gesture toward the car.

Cole took a short leather cord out of his pocket and tied his hair back into a tail to keep it out of his face while he worked. The end hung down between his shoulder blades.

He approached the car from the sidewalk to keep his shadow off it. Hess's guys sure did a job on her: flat tires, shattered windows, bullet holes in the quarter panel and hood. He opened the driver's side door and the dome light came on. No blood on the seat, or anywhere else on the interior that he could see. He slipped inside.

A barrage of scents struck him: the fake new car smell the detailers used between rentals; the stale cigarette smoke lingering in the ceiling fabric; the rotten bits of food the vacuum missed between the seat and the console; the hint of cocoa butter-infused hotel shampoo in the headrest. That last had to be Agent Wallace, or the cleansers would have overwhelmed it.

Now he had her scent. If only he could read her intent as easily.

FOUR

SEAN THREW TWO QUICK, SHORT JABS into his opponent's face. Not enough to do any harm, but enough to make Max bring his hands up to a guard position. Sean shot in low for a double-leg takedown, shoved forward and put Max flat on his back. A quick scramble and he had mount, straddling Max's hips with his knees. Max turtled up to avoid the inevitable rain of blows to the head, and Sean popped him a good one in the gut.

"Ding, ding, ding!" Dustin called from the sideline. He ran in and got between the two fighters.

Sean jumped to his feet and backed away. Max went limp and lay spread-eagle on the mat, chest heaving for breath. He spat out his mouthguard and let it roll down the side of his face, leaving a trail of spittle down his cheek.

A good promoter would not have predicted any other outcome. On paper, Max would get the nod. Neither man had any fights under his belt, and while both stood around five feet nine, Max fought two weight classes higher and should have the advantage. But Sean, lean but not ripped, walked around at his fighting weight, while Max had to diet and sweat down a good ten pounds to make weight. Sean moved with grace and energy, and his youthful exuberance was reflected in his reddish-brown skin and spiky black hair. Max's movements were slow and deliberate, and a steady diet of beer and cheeseburgers left him with thick love handles, and a complete lack of muscle definition.

Dustin knelt down beside Max and flashed him the middle finger. "You alright? How many fingers am I holding up?"

Max tried to laugh, but it came out a dry wheeze. "Bastard."

"Yeah, he's alright. I don't know how you do it, Sean. Your cardio's insane!"

"Nah. Max just needs to stop smoking."

"Speaking of," Max said, "let's step outside, eh?"

"See what I mean?" The three of them laughed.

Sean extended a hand to his sparring partner. Dustin took Max's other hand and, together, they helped him to his feet. They took off their gloves and headgear, and Max went to his duffle bag to find his smokes.

"I'm telling you, man, you should think about taking some amateur fights," Dustin said. "I'll put up your fees, we'll put the gym's sponsorship on it, get some more fighters in here. Maybe then we can afford to get some real equipment."

Sean looked around the gym. The Great North Combat Arts Center had a nice ring to it, but while he found it homey, most other wannabes expected more. Dustin built the place in one of his old man's vacant shops, put out a shingle, and hoped the MMA craze would do the rest. They had a range of free weights, a couple of bikes, a treadmill, and two old, used wrestling mats purchased from an area high school. They had tractor tires and sandbags for non-traditional workouts, and their ring consisted of an elevated platform covered by a thin mat. Two sections of chain-link fence formed a partial corner for fighters to do cage work against. The office along the north wall had windows so Dustin could keep an eye on the gym floor while he conducted the business side of things.

A handful of wrestlers came in to work out, as did a few area boneheads who thought they were tough. One of the bar bouncers came in to see what he'd be dealing with from the local wannabes. Enough to keep the lights on and Dustin's dad off his back, but not enough to call it a real business.

Which was a shame because Dustin was no slouch. He carried a 4-1 amateur record as a middleweight, and had a passion for the sport. He had a Judo black belt, and he dabbled in karate and jujutsu while he served with the Marine Corps in Okinawa. Every time he squirreled enough money away, he'd head out to Vegas to train with the pros for a week or so. Lean, chiseled, and still sporting his military high-and-tight haircut, he even looked like a fighter. Maybe there were better coaches out there, but Sean really felt like he was learning a lot from Dustin.

"I wish I could, bro. But you know, family and all."

Max snorted. "You mean brother and all. You need to tell Cole to get off your jock."

"Ah, it's not all his fault. Mom's not crazy about the idea, either. But hey, I'm just here for fun. I bet real fighters would stomp my ass into the mat."

"I don't know, I think the potential's there," Dustin said. "I won't push, but just know, you ever want to take a crack at it, I'm in your corner."

"Yeah, me too," Max said.

"I guess somebody needs to be the water boy." Sean bumped Dustin with an elbow and they both laughed.

Max held up his fist, one cigarette protruding from his knuckles like a middle finger.

"Now come on, you dicks. My nicotine system has too much oxygen in it."

They headed for the door, stopping long enough to step into their boots, but not bothering to lace them. The sweat evaporating off their bodies cooled to water vapor, making it look as though they were on fire. Sean took a deep breath and let the chilly air bite his lungs while Max lit up his cigarette. He was still winded from their sparring and coughed at the first inhale.

"Told you you should quit." Sean turned to Dustin. "Didn't I say he should quit?"

"Yeah, yeah." Max took another puff.

Max started smoking at sixteen, and had been trying to quit since his twenty-second birthday nearly two years ago. Sean never saw the appeal himself. He was glad his friend was finally trying to quit, but at this point he wasn't sure what more he could do to help.

A bright beam of light swept across them, and a small black car idled down the dead-end street between the gym and the next shop over, the Hammer & Lathe. Both buildings shared the corner of a small industrial complex owned by Dustin's father and leased out to various operations. The Hammer & Lathe turned out furniture, shelving, and other carpentry works, and the lights shining from the narrow windows along the roofline indicated someone must be working the late shift.

The car swung into the H&L parking lot and pulled right up to the door. The driver, dressed all in black, got out of the car. Two men came out and greeted him.

"Isn't that Slick?" Dustin asked.

"The driver?" Sean could barely make them out in the light of the street lamp at the end of the lot. "Maybe. I think this is the first I've seen him without his colors."

It was no secret some of the guys belonged to a motorcycle club called Lucifer's Swords. Slick wore their flaming sword-and-skull logo and rocker on both denim and leather, and the way he strutted around ensured everybody noticed. With his long hair, three-inch Van Dyke, and perpetual three-day beard stubble, he looked rough and scuzzy. Sean also realized this was the first he'd seen Slick without his bike, a blacked-out nightmare of a customized Road King.

Slick clasped hands with the first man out the door, Evan Carson. Dustin said a lot of the shop paperwork was in Evan's name, but he didn't seem to do much more than stand around the shop. He was older than most of the other guys, with a thick head of short, salt-and-pepper hair and a healthy beer belly. He carried himself like he was in charge, though, and his coarse hands wore the scars of many a fistfight.

The third man hung back a few feet. Sean didn't recognize him. He stood several inches taller than Slick and Evan, but his gray work shirt hung loose and baggy on his thin frame. He thrust his hands in his pockets and tried to look relaxed, but he kept watching the street and glancing over at Sean and the others.

Their voices carried across the street. Sean couldn't make out the words, but Slick said something like "it's done." A moment later Evan and the thin man went back inside and Slick returned to his car. He looked over at Sean and the others as he opened the door.

"What're you fags staring at?" he shouted. "Shouldn't you be rolling around on the floor together or something?" He laughed and slammed his car door shut.

"Fuckin' douche." Max flicked his cigarette in a high arc toward Slick's car. It threw off embers as it bounced into the street.

"Think it will ever get old for him?" Dustin asked.

"I doubt it. The guy's probably got a memory like a goldfish. Every time he says it, he's hearing it for the first time."

Sean and Max laughed as Slick pulled out of the parking lot. He put the hammer down and raced around the corner and down the street. The revving engine faded into the distance.

"Don't sweat it," Dustin said. "Just be content in the knowledge you could turn him inside out if he had the balls to come over and say it to our faces. Besides, my old man's getting real worried about some of the things they're doing in that shop. They may not be around much longer."

FIVE

THE BITCH SET HER UP.

And Angie fell for it, suckered like a suit fresh out of Quantico.

She should have seen the signs. Hess's dispatcher, Jennifer Mills, didn't seem all that concerned when Angie first showed up looking for the sheriff yesterday. Angie identified herself as a reporter investigating the Tyler family, and Mills politely informed her Sheriff Hess wasn't in, took down her information, and sent her on her way.

Then, this morning, Mills had sat down across from Angie as she pushed a bite of Eggs Benedict through a puddle of chunky Hollandaise sauce.

"Good morning," Angie said.

Mills didn't say anything. She sat low in the booth, and her eyes darted all around the room, stopping for just a second on each of the few patrons in the diner. A blue plaid shirt flattened the curves her uniform had showed off yesterday, and without makeup, her laugh lines and freckles stood out like pocks of rust on a classic Mustang. She had been pretty once, but now it only came with effort. Long strands of stray hair stood out in all directions from her bushy ponytail.

"Can I get you some coffee?"

Mills's focus snapped back to Angie, her eyes wide. A breath later, she relaxed just a little. Nodded, whispered, "Please."

Angie flipped the second mug on the table right side up, then caught the waitress's eye and raised her own mug. Mills looked over her shoulder, watching the waitress head for the counter, then gave Angie a look, that apologetic look that says, "I shouldn't have come here."

The woman had something to say, Angie thought, but something spooked her enough to give her second thoughts. Time to throw her a curveball. Angie held up her fork.

"It amazes me how difficult it is to get this right."

Mills blinked. "What?"

"Hollandaise." Angie popped the bit of food into her mouth, chewed. "Yeah, see, too much lemon juice overpowers the flavor, and when the egg gets overcooked you get lumps. You know the cook?"

"Teddy? Sure."

"Not very patient, is he?"

Mills smiled, and a soft pink flush filled the spaces between her freckles. Yeah, she knew him, alright. If not a recent relationship, then at least a fling in their youth and a fond memory.

The waitress arrived with two pots of coffee. A skinny young thing with piercings in her eyebrow and lip, she topped Angie's cup off with regular. Mills asked for the same, then declined a menu. The waitress shrugged and took her coffee to another table.

"Are you sure you're not hungry?" Angie asked. "It's on me."

"No, thank you. I need to go soon. I just . . ."

Angie reached across and set her hand on Mills's wrist. Mills flinched, but did not withdraw her hand.

"Whatever you have to say, it's just between the two of us. I swear."

Mills's lip trembled. She blinked and looked away.

It must be juicy, Angie thought. She waited a moment while Mills composed herself, wiping her eye with her free hand.

"It's the sheriff," Mills said at last. She glanced around, then leaned in close, spoke in a soft murmur. "He's . . . done things. Illegal things. Those men you asked about? Marcus Rice and Will Tyler? That was all his fault."

"How so?"

Mills shook her head. "Not here. I shouldn't be seen with you. The sheriff, he has a temper. We need to meet somewhere else."

"Did Hess kill Will Tyler?"

"Please. Not here. There's a deserted town not far from here. A place called Charity. We can meet there this evening."

"Come on, you can't give me just a taste?"

"No, it's too dangerous. You don't know who's listening. I'm already taking a big risk sitting with you like this."

"No."

Mills's eyes went wide. "What?"

"How do I know you're not yanking my chain? If you're going to tell me where the sheriff's bodies are buried, why not now? Why not in my hotel room, or a quiet spot in town?"

"But—"

"If you've got info for me, great, but I'm not going to jump through hoops to get it. Have a nice day." Angie went back to her breakfast. It was a calculated risk, but if Mills really wanted to spill her guts, she would.

Mills sank into her seat. She went to speak, then stopped. She pulled her purse into her lap, and for a moment Angie thought she really would leave.

Then she looked around once more, leaned across the table, and whispered "Wouldn't you rather just see where the bodies are buried?"

Hook, line and sinker.

Angie wondered whom Mills feared most: herself or Sheriff Hess. Had Hess put her up to getting Angie out here, or was Mills in on the ambush from the beginning?

She would be sure to find out when she got back to Sunset, and then she'd call in some heavy artillery. She would catch hell from the Bureau, but at least she would be closer to some real answers.

The Bureau had found no real links between Rod Babineaux and the Tylers or Nevada, and they saw no reason to reopen the investigations into the deaths of Will Tyler or Kate Henrikssen. Yet it bugged Angie that a week after their disappearance Cole Tyler could shoot out here and put it all together, then come home with the bodies. The Tylers had to be hiding something out here. Something big. The doctors had yet to clear her for fieldwork, so she burned some vacation time and came out to do a little sniffing around.

Now she'd stepped in a big pile of stink. Her own damned stubbornness may just get her killed.

After the sun went down, the temperature dropped fast. Angie rubbed her arms to ward off the chill. She wore a light jacket in anticipation of the cooler evening, but now wished she had put a sweatshirt on underneath. She drew her pistol and approached the front window.

An overcast night left the town in near total darkness. She could make out the houses across the street and the borders of the streets themselves, but the finer details were lost on her. It could work out in her favor, provided her assailants didn't pack night vision gear or bring dogs.

She tested the front door. The handle turned, but the deadbolt had seized shut. She went back through the house to the back door and listened.

Silence.

No sounds of desert animal nightlife, no motion, no lights.

Part of her still wanted to hole up in the house, stay hidden until someone could come looking for her. But who? She hadn't told anybody where she was going, and because she was on leave, nobody at the office would be worried about her for at least a few more days. If Hess's men were as determined as she'd feared, it would only be a matter of time before they found her.

She considered striking out across the desert, find a home or another town, and make a few phone calls. Even if she could keep her bearings, there was no telling how far the nearest shelter would be, and she wouldn't last long on foot without water.

Her only real option was to find a car, then get back to town and get on a phone. With her car toast, she'd have to get her hands on one of the bad guys' rides. Taking the fight to them felt like suicide, but it beat baking to death in the desert or waiting until they flushed her out.

She took a deep breath, let it out slow, then stepped out into the backyard.

SIX

RONNIE PULLED AMY IN TIGHTER, ground against her pelvis a little harder. She cooed in response, and her fingernails raked across his shoulders. She nibbled his ear just the way he liked it, and he pumped faster. She moaned, then bit her lip and made that cute little squeak she made every time she came but wanted to suppress the noise. She squeaked higher, louder, and with a grunt and one more powerful thrust, he buried himself deep and released. Amy shuddered beneath him, and they both collapsed into the bed, Ronnie careful to keep his weight on his elbows, lest he crush her.

They laid together like that for a moment, breathing heavily while their sweat glued their bodies together. Then Ronnie felt hot. He rolled off of her to one side of the bed, brushed his hair out of his eyes and behind his ear. Amy rolled after him and laid her cheek on his shoulder. It still felt hot and sticky, but he liked the feel of her small breasts crushed against his side. She traced the line down the middle of his abs with a fingertip.

"You should come to my place," she said. "I can make us dinner, and we can take our time together. We'll have a real date for once, not just one of these secret little quickies."

"That reminds me, we best get back to it." Ronnie slipped away from her and kicked his legs over the side of the bed, stood up.

"Is that a no?"

Ronnie looked back at her in the dim light thrown from the small lamp near the cabin's front door. She smiled, but he could see the hurt in her eyes.

"Do you think it's a good idea?"

She shrugged. "My neighbors keep to themselves. Nobody's going to rat us out."

"That's not what I meant."

"Oh." She jumped out of bed on the other side and picked up her panties.

Ronnie watched her dress as he put on his own clothes. She had a nice, tight ass, a trim figure, and a flat belly. He normally didn't care for short hair on a woman, but her bob cut flattered her delicate features. Twenty-two, smoking hot, no husband and no kids. She took care of herself, worked out. He felt like maybe she earned his desire.

Not like Kate. Will's girlfriend was too soft, too sweet for Ronnie's taste. But Will loved her, though, and it was good to see Will happy for as long as it had lasted.

"You're probably right." Amy turned around as she tucked her red Tyler Lodge polo shirt into her black slacks. "I mean, we've only known one another a few weeks. Sure, I like you and all, but I know how it is. I don't want to go screwing things up between you and your mom, or her to feel like I'll file a harassment claim on you guys."

They would make a good pair, of course. Physically. Combine his height, his slim build, broad shoulders and narrow waist, with her tight little bod, and they would produce some solid little kids. They'd be handsome devils, too.

But there were a whole lot of things to be considered before they could go that far.

As she spoke, Ronnie finished tying his hiking boots. He stood and walked over to her.

"Maybe we should slow down," she said. "Maybe we should stop and think about . . . what're you . . . ?"

He slipped a hand around the small of her back, pulled her in close, then bit the side of her neck. Just a nibble, enough to make her stiffen up and suck air through her teeth. She then relaxed against him until he broke it off.

"I don't know why, but that really turns me on," Amy cooed.

"We'll talk about it another time," he said.

"The biting?"

"Hitting your place."

"Oh. Yeah, okay."

"Good. You'd best finish this cabin before my mom comes looking for you. I'm going to finish my rounds."

Ronnie kissed her on the forehead. She said good night, and he opened the front door a crack, peered out at the road and campsite, then went outside. He heard Amy's vacuum kick on as he walked past the old Cherokee they kept stocked with cleaning supplies and fresh linens.

Amy did good work. He'd hate to see Mom fire her because he'd let her get too close and risk a repeat of what happened to Kate.

Ronnie jogged the couple hundred yards to the next campsite where he'd left the pickup truck. When he opened the driver's side door, his mother's voice greeted him from the radio.

"Ronnie, have you got your ears on out there? Where are you?"

"Shit." He grabbed the handset and keyed the mic. "I'm here, Ma. What's up?"

"Where have you been? I've been trying to raise you for five minutes."

"Sorry, I was tied up with some campers." Tied up? he thought. Maybe next time.

"Can you take the Hayes group out to the east side tonight and get them set up?"

"I thought Cole was handling that."

"He's not going to be around a while. I need you to do it."

"What do you mean 'not going to be around?' What's going on?"

A pause. "We'll talk about it later. Are you going to do the job or not?"

In other words, she can't talk about it on the radio. The plastic handset squeaked and crackled in Ronnie's grip. Now what kind of trouble had Cole gotten into? After a second, he relaxed his grip and took a deep breath.

"I haven't finished my rounds yet," he said.

"They can keep until Sean gets back."

"Alright. I'm on it, Ma."

"Thanks, hon. Base out."

"Yeah." He threw the handset back into the cab, then climbed in and started the engine.

This must have something to do with why Cole was so edgy last night, and why he'd been gone all day today. Any time Ronnie has a beef, big brother Cole's quick to remind him they're a family and have to go work together. Yet, every time something's up, Cole races off on his own to handle it.

And that just worked out so well last time. Ronnie punched the steering wheel. Yeah, they'd be talking about it later, alright.

Maybe Diana had the right idea. None of them wanted their baby sis to leave at the time, especially Cole. He insisted the wounds of Will's death were too fresh, that nobody should make any rash decisions. Mom finally relented, though, and they packed Diana off to college the following summer.

"Illinois isn't all that far," Mom had reasoned. Funny how Diana always found some excuse not to come home during most of her breaks. A trip with friends. Summer studies. A job or an internship.

Whether it was just a part of college life or an intentional dodge of family drama didn't matter; she'd escaped. Ronnie had no intention of going back to school himself, but more and more he envied her for it.

SEVEN

"YOU DON'T GET SHIT until I see some green." Evan crossed his arms and scowled at the three kids standing in front of him. The dingy light in the alley behind the club gave their faces a sickly orange pallor. The place reeked of piss and trash, and an incessant bass thump radiated through the brick wall, rattling the Dumpster.

"A hundo's a bit steep, brah. We're used to payin' fiddy." The kid on the left tried to look tough with his white hoodie adorned with nonsensical, faux-tribal MMA designs and the ring through his lower lip, but he couldn't take his eyes off the colorful tattoo adorning Evan's left forearm. The ornate sword wreathed in bright orange and yellow flames made a good eye-catcher, and the scroll ribbon reading *Lucifer's Swords, M.C.* cemented the effect.

Hoodie's boy stood to the right. He wore a downy vest and a backwards ball cap with the price tag still hanging from one of the vent holes. His left hand twitched several times a second. His hollow cheeks and wide eyes gave him a haunted look. Every time Evan so much as glanced at him, his gaze darted to the asphalt.

The girl standing behind them looked a bit younger, maybe nineteen. A bit too chunky for the heels and hose she sported, and a bit too clean for the likes of these clowns. Maybe she liked the bad boys, carried a rebellious grudge against a rich daddy. Evan had seen the type over and over.

"This isn't the backwoods crank those Nazi wannabes used to sell you. You want a fifty-dollar hit, don't come complaining to me when it burns your brain right outta your skull. What I'm offering here is grade A, made from the finest ingredients. A hundred is just our low-low introductory price for a ride you'll never forget."

Hoodie snorted. "That's what they all say."

"You calling me a liar, kid?" Evan's eyes narrowed into a practiced glare.

"Nah, man. C'mon." Hoodie stepped back, trying to keep up that outward cool but ready to bolt if Evan so much as made a fist. "It's just, you know, first taste is free, right?"

"Not in my business plan, kid. Product speaks for itself."

"Just give it to him," Twitch whispered.

"Man, I'm try'n a . . ." Hoodie looked about to backhand his boy, but held it back.

Trying to negotiate? Evan cracked a smile, then killed it. Not a prayer, shitbird.

"Alright, look. Can we meet halfway? Seventy-five."

"A hundred bucks. Take it or leave it."

"C'mon, Teddy!" Twitch pleaded. "Just give it to him!"

The wind went right out of Hoodie's sails. With a resigned sigh, he reached into his baggy pants, pulled out a folded stack of bills. Counted off five and passed them over.

Evan turned the bills toward the light and made sure they were all twenties, then pocketed them. He reached back and knocked on the club's back door twice, short and sharp.

Half a second later the door opened. Loud music and the murmur of the crowd spilled out, followed by Evan's man Sid, another Chicago import for the MC's new home in Emington. He ditched his cut in favor of a red flannel shirt with the sleeves rolled up over a black knit sweatshirt in an effort to keep a low profile for now. Sweat dotted his bald head, and he scowled through his thick goatee.

"Give me a single," Evan said.

Sid passed over a small plastic baggie and disappeared back into the club. The bass dropped to a dull throb. Evan held the bag out toward Twitch.

Twitch snatched it and worked it open with his thumbs. He pressed the small opening to his left nostril and inhaled deeply.

"Hey, wait, man! Why'd you give it to him?" Hoodie asked.

"Because if my partner accidentally handed me the wrong bag, your buddy here just got a snoot full of ground glass."

Hoodie and the chunky girl gasped, but Twitch had already landed in La La Land. His eyes rolled up into his head and he leaned against the wall for support.

"Well?" Hoodie asked.

"This . . . This is good shit." Twitch smiled and rubbed his crotch.

"What the hell is he doing?" The girl had a hint of disgust in her voice.

"That'd be the kick," Evan said. "We've got a little something extra tickles the back of your brain, the animal part that controls your instincts. In a few minutes, your man here will be ready to fuck a hole in that wall."

"Dude, we'll take more." Hoodie turned to the girl. "How much you got?"

"I don't know about this, Teddy."

"Bitch, don't start! Just give me the money!"

Hoodie grabbed her purse. She clutched it tighter to her side, and he started yanking on it.

"Stop it, Teddy! That hurts!"

Hoodie held up a fist. "I will pop you in the fuckin' mouth if you don't come up with the cash!"

Fuck it, Evan thought. He grabbed Hoodie's wrist, yanked it down. Just as Hoodie turned his head to see what was happening, he caught Evan's right cross smack in the center of his face. His head snapped back and his knees buckled. Evan held onto the kid's arm as he hit the ground, then kicked him in the ribs.

"Stop it!" the girl screamed. "You're hurting him!"

"That's the idea, skank." Evan kicked Hoodie in the ribs again, then glanced over at Twitch. The kid just grunted and licked his lips, and stared at the girl's legs. Evan turned back to Hoodie and put a toe kick into his back. Hoodie screamed and arched his back.

"Here!" The girl rummaged through her purse, came up with some money. She tried to count it, then just thrust it at Evan. "Take it! We'll buy some! Just, please, leave him alone!"

Evan tilted up his chin, considered it. Tears poured from the girl's eyes. Hoodie gagged once, then threw up. Orange muck spilled all over the asphalt and splashed his hands.

Evan took the money, counted it, pocketed it. He summoned Sid again, got a larger bag, and tossed it to the girl. It hit her chest, then the ground, but she bent over and picked it up.

"Now get this worthless sack of shit out of my sight." He grabbed Twitch, yanked him up to his feet and hurled him toward the girl. "This one, too."

Hoodie and the girl rushed down the alley, almost dragging Twitch as they went. Evan and Sid watched them go until they hit the sidewalk and turned the corner.

"What was that about?" Sid asked.

"Just having a little fun."

"Hell of a way to treat new customers."

"Ah, they'll be back after they get a good taste."

"It's not sales I'm worried about."

"Goddamn it, Sid, just speak your mind already!"

Sid looked down for a moment.

"Whatever you're thinking, it ain't written in the asphalt."

"It's the cops, man. They catch these kids with our junk, how long is it gonna take for them to give us up? We keep roughing them up, they'll sing first chance they get."

"So what? How is it different from any other time we sling?" Evan shook his head. "This isn't the time to grow a pussy, you know. We have work to do."

Sid stepped in close, spoke low. "And we're also cutting out the competition, so to speak. How long do you think it'll take the local law to put it together?"

"That's my problem, not yours. Now back out of my face before I have to do something you regret."

Sid's upper lip twitched. Not quite a snarl, but he thought about it. He had several inches on Evan, both in height and shoulder breadth, but Evan wouldn't hesitate to put him down hard and fast.

"I'm just looking out for the club, that's all," Sid said. The only way to save face.

"Fair enough," Evan said. "Again, my problem. I don't make this happen, we all go down. Now, you got anything left?"

"We're tapped out, boss. Just a couple of singles."

"Good. Hand them out and I'll meet you back at the Hammer."

"You got it." Sid went back inside.

Evan walked down the alley in the opposite direction he'd sent the kids. He pulled a smoke out of the pack in his breast pocket and lit up. Sure, maybe he pushed a little too hard, but tonight they'd moved more product than any night so far, and they'd eliminated the last of their competition. All in all, he had to call that a win.

He still hated it here. He'd been excited when he'd first been tapped to start a new chapter, but when they told him where, he thought they were joking. Why some podunk burg in the middle of nowhere? He could see Minneapolis, and people had at least heard of Fargo, but he just didn't see the sense of this place.

And insult to injury, the riding season here was even shorter than back home.

Not that he had a choice in the matter. When the club said jump, he jumped. If they wanted an Emington chapter, they'd damn well get one, and it would be the best-run chapter in the whole club. All the higher-ups would know his name, and then he'd start getting some recognition.

All he needed now was to get their attention.

EIGHT

THE HARDWOOD FLOOR CRACKED and groaned as Harvey slipped down the hall and into the kitchen. He swept the shotgun barrel left and right through the kitchen, then nudged the back door open and peered outside. Then he relaxed his shoulders and stepped back into the kitchen.

"This is ridiculous," he said. "There have to be a hundred houses on this street alone. We could have passed her three times and never known it!"

"Not very likely," Cole said.

"Why do you say that?"

"Because if she knows your cars are the only ticket out of here, she'll be looking for us same as we're looking for her."

"How dangerous is she?"

Cole shrugged. "How dangerous would you be if someone took a shot at you and hunted you through an old ghost town?"

"No, man, I mean how well do you know this chick? Are we going to be able to take her down, or do we have a real problem?"

"She's the sole survivor of a massacre in which over a dozen people died."

"Wonderful."

Cole couldn't help but smile in the darkness. He peered out a nearby window and scanned the surrounding yard and houses.

"You're sure you have no idea what she's doing out here?" Harvey asked.

"Hess told me she asked for any files related to my brother's case, and that's it."

"I hear she rode out to Charlie Rice's old place this afternoon, too."

"Did she find anything?"

"Nah. Ain't nothing to find. We torched the place right after we got rid of Marcus's body. No bodies, no DNA, no nothing." Harvey looked out the window for a moment, then turned toward Cole. "Look, Tyler, I need to know you're going to do the right thing, here."

Cole couldn't quite make out Harvey's expression, but he heard the squeak of plastic and rubber as the deputy's grip tightened around the grip of his shotgun.

"Don't sweat it," Cole said. "I don't make the same mistake twice."

Silence as Harvey mulled that over for a moment.

"Good," Harvey said at last. "I ain't going to jail for that bitch."

"Then I guess we'd better keep moving." Cole pushed past the deputy and went out the back door.

A cool breeze wafted across his face. He inhaled deeply through his nose. A cacophony of scents greeted him, everything from the tang of the earth beneath his feet to the decaying wood all around them. He picked up the mark of a desert coyote, as well as the remains of what could have been its latest meal. Not a hint of Wallace's shampoo.

They crept across the yard toward the adjacent lot behind it. A flimsy metal shed groaned in the wind as they passed, and something tiny scurried out of Cole's path. He watched the windows for any sign of movement, and scanned the corners of the house for anyone that might be watching them.

Nothing.

The screen door of the next house lay on the ground beside the walk. Half of the back door hung loose from the hinges, and half of the remainder had been scattered across the kitchen. Most of the linoleum on the other side of the threshold was peeled away, exposing the cracked and brittle subfloor. It gave lightly beneath Cole's weight, and he used tentative steps to find the floor joists to walk on.

He sniffed the air. More dry and decaying wood. The bitter stench of the vegetation creeping up the wall near the window. A faint chemical scent, probably related to the broken glass and plastic on the floor and countertops.

No Wallace.

Cole stepped aside for Harvey. Harvey crept through the room and to the next doorway, whipped his shotgun around the corner, then slipped into the room. Cole listened as the deputy's footsteps moved through the house.

Cole could hear his brother's voice in the back of his head: *Kill them all.* Shift, hunt down everyone involved, and take them down.

If only it could be that simple. Unfortunately, there were too many variables. How many people were involved? What about the bodies? What about the paper trails of Agent Wallace's trip, or his own? Who would be the next person to come looking for answers, to start sniffing around Sunset or the lodge? The dead may not spill their secrets, but they tended to leave plenty of clues behind. That made the beast a great tool for burying secrets, but it tended to leave even more clues in its wake.

Just like last fall. They kept the family secret, yet here came Agent Wallace, digging up those clues.

Harvey's radio crackled in the next room. A moment later the deputy returned.

"The rest of the backup's arrived," he said. "This should make things easier."

"How many of them know what's really going on here?" Cole asked.

"What do you mean?"

"How many of them know Wallace is a fed, or about the Rices and my brother?"

"Oh. I don't know, probably a few. Depends who Jerry called. Why?"

Shit. More clues and loose ends.

"I just don't want this to get out of hand," Cole said. "This may be more than even the sheriff can handle."

"Don't you worry about that. Sunset's got its own way of solving its problems, and Sheriff Hess, he'll make this work."

By generating more bodies. That didn't make the sheriff any better than the beast. Cole long suspected Will wasn't the first "problem" Hess solved with a bullet. How many other bodies had he and his men buried at the mine, or out in the desert?

"Then, let's get a move on," Cole said. "I want to find her before someone else gets trigger-happy."

NINE

ANGIE STOPPED BETWEEN two dilapidated homes to stretch her quads and relieve the tension seizing her aching hip. Damned thing slowed her down more than she expected. Insult to injury, it made her lazy, made her fat. She may not tip the scales a whole lot higher than before she took the bullet, but she could certainly pinch a bigger fold of skin across her belly, and her hips tugged her jeans taut. Little things nobody would notice but her, but enough to irritate the shit out of her.

She knew she couldn't have covered more than a few blocks when she first fled the ambush, but she'd just covered at least twice that distance with no sign of her attackers, her disabled car, or even the downtown area. She must have gotten turned around somewhere, most likely where the street took an abrupt turn.

It didn't help that the desert sand and wind had scoured most of the street signs clean. If she could locate Main Street, one way or the other, it would get her to a reference point she could use to find a car. She looked up and down the street one more time, then decided to check the next block to see if she couldn't find a better perspective.

She went to the backyard and walked along a wooden fence running the perimeter of the yard to her left. She walked around a cluster of metal posts sticking up out of a long-dead garden, crossed to the next yard and walked between a pair of old picnic tables.

The back door of the house in front of her opened with a loud creak.

Angie dropped to the ground and wriggled beneath the table. A tall figure with a long gun stepped onto the stoop, then down to the yard. She brought her pistol around in front of her, careful to keep it low to the ground. The tall man moved through the yard to her right, his body facing the other direction.

A second man came out the door, this one a little shorter and dressed all in black, with a short, chunky handgun in his right hand. He pulled the door shut behind him and walked over to his partner.

"What do you think?" the man in black asked.

"Let's try this one." The tall man gestured toward the home next door with his shotgun.

"Works for me."

The two of them started toward the next house. Angie watched them go a few more yards until they reached an overgrown driveway running from the garage to her right to the street out front. They ignored the garage and its collapsed roof.

Angie rolled out from under the table, wincing at the soft whisper of her jacket against the desert dirt. The two men didn't give any sign they heard her, though, and she pushed herself up to her feet and moved to the middle of the yard. She thumbed back the hammer on her pistol, the metallic snap loud and sharp in the quiet night.

"Freeze." She kept her voice low. Cool as ice.

The men stiffened.

"Let's not do anything stupid, lady," the taller man said.

"Put your guns down and put your hands on your heads." She moved a few steps closer, kept her gun trained on the taller man's back. Neither of them looked like the man she'd shot. How many of them are there now? A chill ran down her back, as she half expected a rifle barrel to poke her spine.

"I don't think you realize how much trouble you're in." He tried to look over his shoulder at her.

"I'm a federal agent. Put your guns on the ground and put your hands on your head, now." With no cuffs or binders, the threat felt hollow.

"We know that's bullshit. Now how about you make this easy and give me that gun before you hurt someone?"

"Oh my God, she's going to shoot us, Hank!" the shorter man whispered, his voice pinched and urgent.

"Like hell she is. She knows one shot will bring our friends running, and shooting." Hank turned toward her halfway. "If she hands me that pistol and comes along all peaceful-like, she just might live. What do you say, lady?"

"Put your guns on the ground. I won't ask again." She stepped closer to the men and to her left to stay behind Hank. He tried to find her again over his opposite shoulder.

"Last chance, la—"

"Shut your mouth!" she snapped. Shorty flinched. He'd disarm easy enough if she could keep Hank quiet. Just a few feet behind them now, she spoke directly to Shorty. "Put your hands up."

Shorty groaned, but he did as he was told. Angie trained her SIG on the center of his back and reached for his handgun.

Hank spun. Angie stepped inside the arc as he swung his rifle butt at her, then blocked his forearm and elbow with both of her own forearms. She struck him just below the ear with the heel of her palm, then kicked him in the back if the knee. He dropped, first hitting his knee, then falling to all fours.

Shorty turned, mouth agape. He brought his hands down, extended his pistol toward Angie. He hesitated.

Angie didn't. She put two rounds into him, one into his chest and the other through his throat. He hit the ground spread-eagle and didn't move. A gurgling sound escaped his throat.

Hank swept her legs out from under her. She tucked her chin and rolled into the fall. The impact stung, but she recovered in time to squirm left and dodge Hank's rifle butt. It slammed into the ground just an inch from her right ear. She reached up through his arms and jammed the muzzle of her pistol into the soft flesh beneath his jaw.

"Fuck," he said.

"Drop it." She spoke through gritted teeth. It took every bit of her restraint to not pull the trigger and splatter him all over the desert.

He leaned back just enough to take the pressure off his jaw. He spread his arms wide, set the shotgun butt on the ground and let it go. It fell away from them, hitting the ground with a clatter.

"Now get up and step back." She had to move fast. His backup would arrive any second. With luck, he had a car nearby.

"Who's shooting? What's happening?" Shorty's jacket muffled the radio clipped to his belt. Angie looked over at the sound, anxious to hear any hint they'd found her or were nearby.

Hank twisted and lashed out with his left hand. His fingers wrapped tight around her wrist as he shoved her arm and pistol away from his jaw. She had just enough time to think, *Idiot*, before his right fist smacked her just below her nose.

The world exploded in a flash of light, then went black. She lost track of the ground and everything spun. Her thoughts went cloudy and impenetrable. What happened? Where am I?

A foreign hand on her SIG snapped her back to the present. She grasped it with both hands and resisted the pull. It all came back in a rush: the desert, a gunfight, a man on top of her.

A man with a clear strength advantage. The gun started to slip through her fingers. He chuckled. Patient, confident in his strength. She threw a knee into his ribs. He grunted and loosened up just enough for her to regain her grip. She kneed him again, and he muttered a curse.

He punched her in the face, a quick jab connecting high on her right cheekbone.

Not as hard as the first, but enough to snap her head around. She kept a death grip on the pistol, and he punched her square in the nose. Fire filled her nose and tears filled her eyes.

She knew she couldn't take much more of that. She did a crunch, pulling herself up to hide her face behind the gun and their entwined, struggling hands. She aimed a kick higher, connected instead with the front of his leg as he threw it over her. He landed hard, straddling her and pinning her hips to the ground. She tried another knee and her thigh thudded against his back, little more than a nuisance.

"Just give it up," he said. "You ain't near strong enough."

Her forearms and biceps ached with the effort. The gun got another inch away from her.

"Let go now, maybe I won't make you eat this gun. Maybe I won't punch all your teeth out before the sheriff gets here."

He peeled her little finger off the barrel, went to work on the others. Her grip started to give.

"That's it. You just give it to ol' Hank and everything will be fine. I promise!"

Maybe he wasn't lying. Maybe . . . No! She craned her head forward and bit his hand. He winced, hissed. She felt his flesh give, tasted blood. His? Hers? It didn't matter. She bit as hard as she could, tried to make her teeth touch.

He grunted hard against the pain. His grip faltered, then at last he cried out and pulled his hands away, leaving flesh in her teeth. Her shoulders fell back to the ground, and she cradled the gun to her chest as he knelt straight up and clutched his bitten hand.

Angie spat out the meat and jammed the gun into his waist. His eyes went wide. She pulled the trigger twice, then once more for good measure. Blood sprayed over her hands, and he doubled over on top of her. She rolled him and he went over easy, screaming and trying to hold his guts together. One more kick and she was out from under him. She braced her boot against his shoulder, shoved him away, extended her arm.

Blam! The shot struck the upper curve of his forehead and blew the top of his skull apart.

Angie collapsed to the ground, heaving for breath. Her arms trembled.

"Talk to me, Phil. Where are you?" The voice on the radio faded in. She heard shouting, too. Far enough she couldn't make out the words, but close enough they'd find her before long.

Angie stood and licked blood off her lip, spat it out. She holstered her SIG, then picked up Shorty's revolver and shoved it in her front pocket. A quick pat-down turned up two full speed loaders, the handheld radio, and a wallet. No keys or cell phone. The speed loaders went into her jacket pocket and the radio to her waistband; she tossed the wallet aside.

A quick search of Hank's body turned up a handful of shotgun shells, a folding knife, and his wallet. Once again no keys, no cell phone.

"Phil? Hank? Where are you?" a man shouted. He had to be just down the street.

Angie left the wallet and pocketed the rest, then picked up the shotgun. She duck-walked along the fence to the next yard, then ran.

TEN

WHEN THE CUSTOMER WALKED OUT of the office Nina slumped her head down on the reception counter. With luck, that would be the last customer complaint of the evening. It had been a long day with Cole gone. Maybe it was time to bring on another office worker, even a part-timer, if only for days like this.

Not that this guy had been all that difficult. He just wanted to get his laptop online, and he was friendly about it. Funny how people came out to the lodge to get away from things, only to bring all their work and stresses with them.

He'd even flirted with her a little, which always surprised her given she'd mourned her fiftieth birthday last year. Time was a lot of the customers flirted with her, particularly the Midwesterners who thought her red skin and raven hair "exotic." Now laugh lines and crow's feet marred her pretty, round face, and a pair of white streaks set off the front of that raven hair. Amy and the other girls insisted she looked much younger, but the few customers who bothered to flirt with her were invariably closer to her own age, or were quite a bit older.

Nina went back to her desk behind the counter to finish counting up the day's receipts. She recorded the numbers in her paper ledger, then put the cash in a small bank deposit bag.

The front door burst open again. She flinched and looked up to see Ronnie storm through, fuming.

"So where is he?" Ronnie slammed the door behind him and leaned across the reception counter.

Nina looked up at him, kept her expression neutral. After a moment, she zipped up the deposit bag, locked it, and spun her chair away from her son to drop the bag in the safe in the back corner.

"Mister Daly is in the lobby," she said. "He says something is wrong with our Wi-Fi."

"There's always something wrong with the Wi-Fi. Where's Cole?"

Nina closed the safe and spun the dial, then stood and hitched up her pants a bit. She smoothed her black lodge polo over the soft layer of flab around her belly and sides, a self-conscious habit she wished she could kick. She crossed her arms and regarded Ronnie through narrowed eyes.

She had to look up to do it. Even in thick-soled hikers, she barely reached his chin. Cole and Ronnie had inherited their father's height, no doubt about it. Ronnie even looked a bit like John, especially around the eyes.

He cocked his head toward her, as if to say, "Well? I'm waiting?"

If she didn't tell him—or worse, she refused—he would go berserk. If she did tell him, he would still be pissed, but then it would be an issue of trust, and he had to find out eventually. Best get it done now.

"Nevada."

Ronnie did the math in his head. "In Sunset? You've gotta be shitting me, Ma!"

"Don't forget who you're talking to."

Ronnie slammed one hand on the counter. He took a deep breath to steady his voice. "What's he doing in Nevada?"

"Sheriff Hess called and warned him Agent Wallace is there, asking a lot of questions."

"What? Why? Because of the bullshit Lars dropped on her? That has nothing to do with the gunrunners! The lawyer said that case was closed!"

"That's what your brother's gone out there to find out."

Ronnie chuckled. "You should have sent us both, Ma."

"Why's that? You think you can do better?"

"You're damned right I could! If he hadn't—"

Nina crossed the room in a blink, leaned over the counter and slapped him across the face. It sounded like a shot in the confines of the small office, and Ronnie pressed a hand to his already-burning cheek.

"You watch your tone, right now. Whatever you may think of the decision, I am still your mother."

"I just don't think it was wise for him to go alone." He spoke through gritted teeth, his fist balled at his side as he backed away from her.

"Your brother knows what he's doing. Just relax, he'll handle it."

"Right, because he handled it so well the last time."

"He handled it just fine last time." Nina glanced at the door, then lowered her voice. "Do you really think things would have turned out any better if he'd killed the sheriff?"

"The sheriff sure as hell wouldn't be around to answer to Agent Wallace."

"No, but we'd have had law enforcement coming at us with everything they have. You think they would've shrugged off the death of a sheriff and one of his deputies, on top of the civilian deaths? Fact is we needed Hess alive to keep things quiet, and thankfully your brother realized that. It's the call that had to be made, and we have to live with it.

"Now let him be while he checks things out. You may not see eye to eye with your brother, but he knows he can count on you. If he needs you, he will call you."

"So it's run and hide, as usual."

"It's not about hiding, Ronnie. It's about surviving. We're not murderers."

"Now you sound just like him. You say we're not murderers, but what do you call what we did to those skinheads? It's not murder just because you and Cole say so? Call it what you want, but as far as I'm concerned this is a chance to fix both of his foul-ups at once."

Before she could respond Ronnie went into the hallway and pulled the door closed behind him. Nina sat down and breathed a heavy sigh. For the first time, she wondered if Ronnie might be right.

ELEVEN

DUSTIN WROTE THE CHECK to the electric company, then entered the amount into his ledger book and crunched the numbers. Another month of barely breaking even. He leaned back across the back of his chair and stretched. It would sure be nice to start drawing a salary from the place.

He turned off the goose-necked desk lamp, plunging the room into darkness. He stood, walked the three paces to his narrow cot, and sat down on the edge. The eight by ten space was intended to be a storeroom or supply closet, not an office, but it gave Dustin some private space, and a place to crash until he could afford an apartment again.

The main office was much larger, but he reserved it for daily business: signing up students, meeting with vendors, and wooing sponsors and promoters. He kept it neat and strictly professional, with some awards, certificates, and his black belt adorning the walls. It had to impress in a way the gym couldn't quite yet. Most folks in the business could at least recognize the gym's potential, but a cot and a pile of dirty laundry would put everybody off.

If he really wanted to make this work, he had to look serious. Signing up the local thugs, hobbyists, and gym rats kept the lights on, but growth meant attracting talent and sponsorships. Get some pros into the place, win a few purses of his own, earn recognition as a trainer, and it could become something substantial.

If only he could talk Sean into taking a fight. Of all the guys coming through, he had the most potential. Sure, he had talent, but he also didn't have the fear. Most guys swagger in, then get popped in the face a few times and learn they're not near as tough as they thought they were. Sean gave back what he got, and then some.

And he enjoyed it.

He didn't get discouraged when Dustin forced him to tap out three times in a row, he learned from it. Every time they rolled, Dustin could see the improvement in him and knew it wouldn't be long before Sean showed some real skill on the ground. A couple more months of training and he could be a formidable fighter, especially starting out on the amateur circuit.

But Sean's excuses just didn't make sense to Dustin. Sean kept blaming his brother and his mom for not letting him fight, but he would never say why. Dustin offered to talk to them about it, show them the fight statistics, show them some footage and explain the rules and laws protecting fighters, but Sean declined every time. Dustin offered to send him to a sports physician for a full physical, on the club's dime—zero obligation—just to allay any medical fears. Again Sean refused.

There had to be something more, something Sean was afraid of or just not willing to talk about. Fear of failure, maybe? Performance anxiety that could make him freeze up in the ring and make him look bad?

Maybe he should talk to Sean about it more directly. Maybe set up a full-contact match, let Sean experience a round of the real thing, show him it's not so bad. Maybe up his training intensity bit by bit, warming him up to it before he knows it.

Maybe, maybe, maybe. Shit. He could play this game all night and get nowhere.

Maybe he just needed to explain it all to Sean, tell him: "I need your help." Find out how far Sean's friendship really went.

No, that wasn't fair. Guilt wouldn't get him anywhere. He had to help Sean discover his own passion for fighting, and to get past whatever his brother and mother held over him.

He leaned back against the wall for a moment, felt his sweat-dampened shirt paste itself to the drywall. A trickle of sweat ran down his ribs. The damn heater working overtime again. This room needed better ventilation in the worst way.

Dustin stood, stretched, and decided to go out and get some air. He patted the canvas mat on the way through the gym.

"Soon, baby," he said. "We'll get there."

He disarmed the alarm box on the door and pushed it open, then reached down for the rubber doorstop.

"Get the fuck out of here!"

Dustin froze. The shout was close, maybe across the street. Another voice responded, too low for him to hear. The tone was desperate, pleading. Dustin leaned into the gap and peered around the edge of the door.

Slick stood in the Hammer & Lathe parking lot, back in a short-sleeved work shirt and his leather vest adorned with the club colors and patches. Three young men stood around him, all in shabby clothes and work boots. Dustin wondered if they'd just wrapped second shift at the tool and die shop down the street.

"This isn't the time or the place," Slick said. "I have nothing for you. Walk!"

"Look, we got money!" One of the guys advanced on Slick. "Just give us a bag and we're out!"

A bag? Dustin wondered. Bag of what?

"Do I need to use smaller fuckin' words?" Slick cupped his hands around his mouth. "Get. Lost! Go back to the trailer park and pump your sister."

Dustin winced. It didn't look good for Slick. Two of the guys towered over him, and the third had arms capable of twisting the little biker's head off. Dustin wondered if he should intervene, maybe earn a little good will between the gym and the club.

Then again, the little shit had it coming.

"Hey, fuck you, man!" one of the workers snapped. His buddies moved in closer. "We're just trying to do a little business here!"

"Wash your boy's greasy cum out of your ears and listen! There ain't no business here for you!"

Here it comes, Dustin thought. The three workers spread out in a semi-circle around Slick.

"You think you're tough because you're wearing a few patches? You think you'll still be tough with that vest hanging outta your ass?" He reached for Slick.

The knife came out so fast Dustin didn't even see it. Slick twitched, and the worker jumped back, howling and holding his own hand, blood dripping on the asphalt.

Slick took two steps back, his grin gleaming like his blade. "Who's next?"

"He fuckin' cut me, man!" the worker shouted. "He cut me deep!"

The other two shared an uncertain look.

"Well?" Slick asked.

"This ain't the end of this," the workers said. They backed off, leading their wounded friend away.

Slick held his arms out wide. "You know where to find me."

The three men climbed into a huge diesel pickup. It fired up with a loud rumble, and they drove over the curb and into the street. Slick pulled a rag out of his back pocket and wiped his knife while watching them leave. Then he folded the blade and went back into the shop.

Dustin closed the door, set the alarm, and went to his office. He picked up the phone and dialed 9-1-1.

TWELVE

ANGIE STOOD IN WHAT LITTLE MOONLIGHT came in through the bathroom window and leaned in close to the mirror. Blood covered her face, hands, and the front of her jacket. Between the darkness and the blood, she could hardly see anything. She probed the split in her lip with the tip of her tongue, wondered if it might not need a stitch. At least the bleeding seemed to be under control.

Same with her nose. It felt tender to the touch, and she could at least breathe through it now that she snorted back thick gobs of blood and phlegm. She pinched the bridge of her nose and wiggled the cartilage. She decided it would hurt a hell of a lot more if it were broken.

The contusion on her cheekbone felt thick and puffy, and she worried it might still be swelling up. More than anything else, she wished she had an ice pack to keep it down, keep it from obscuring her vision. She didn't need to be creeping around in the dark with one eye. Worst case, maybe she could cut it, drain it herself.

She winced just thinking about it.

Better than the alternative. The two men she left lying in the dirt back there couldn't bitch about anything anymore.

The shorter one—Phil—had been self-defense. She pulled his .44 revolver out of her pocket, and sat down on the closed toilet. She hefted the weapon in her hand. It felt heavy. She could almost put her pinky down the barrel, but it would have put holes many times that size through her if given the chance. Justifiable, no question.

Hank, though . . .

Hank was down. Gutshot, point blank. A man doesn't get up and keep fighting after that.

She told herself it was self-defense. She told herself if he kept screaming, he'd bring the rest of the group down on top of her. She told herself he needed to die.

But she had been so angry. He put a hurt on her, and she wanted him dead. She didn't put two in his chest, center of mass, no Mr. Prosecutor, sir. She shot him right in the fucking face.

If she'd left him alive and screaming, the others would have found him. If they got him to an ER fast enough, he may even have lived. He'd obviously been lied to. Maybe he didn't know the full truth. Maybe he wasn't involved in all of this. Maybe he was just a miserable prick who liked to beat up women.

That didn't mean he deserved to die.

Just a few months ago, she lay bleeding out in the snow, staring up into a gun barrel. She recalled that hopeless feeling, thinking she was about to die and knowing she couldn't do a goddamned thing about it. Why did she deserve to be saved at the last instant? Where was Hank's dramatic rescue?

Her hand trembled as she wiped a tear from the corner of her eye. She looked at it, almost lost in the darkness.

Jesus. Surrounded by armed men hunting for her, and she sat crying on the shitter in an abandoned house.

She stood. Took a deep breath.

Get a grip, Ange! It's just a post-trauma, adrenaline crash. A physiological response, and maybe a little survivor's guilt.

Concentrate on getting out. Survive. Deal with the consequences later. Save the tears for a therapist.

Angie holstered her SIG and shoved the .44 into her waistband at the small of her back. She picked up the shotgun, made sure she had a live round in the chamber, and double-checked the spare shells in her jacket pocket. Then she went to the small room at the front of the house. She looked up the street one way, then down the other.

A car sat in the intersection. She could just make out the profile of the lightbar mounted on the roof. The driver shined a spotlight on the house on the corner, then let it play across the front of the next house. The car backed up, turned down the street toward her. It crept along, shining the spotlight through the windows.

Laziness? she wondered. Or trying to lure her out?

She pressed her back to the wall beside the door and waited. When the car passed the house, she would come up behind them. Some quick shotgun work through the back window and the car would be hers.

Bright white light lanced through the window, played across the tacky wallpaper and crumbling ceiling. Angie shrank even tighter against the wall. She squeezed the shotgun tighter to kill the tremble in her fingers.

The light slipped across the door and into the window on the other side. Dust and cobwebs glittered in the beam. It rolled through the room, then swept away.

Angie allowed her eyes a moment to readjust to the darkness, then looked out through the small windows cut into the door. The car had moved on to the next couple of houses.

She twisted the front door handle. The latch clicked like a shot inside the living room, but the car showed no sign the occupants had heard anything. She opened the door, slow and gentle. The hinges ground across their pins, but not so loud the men in the car would hear anything. She hefted the shotgun, and watched the car through the gap. It rode the center of the street. The driver's side window was down.

"Hey there!" someone shouted.

Angie craned her neck and looked up the street. A tall man with a black shotgun walked into range of the car's headlights. He approached the hood with one arm raised. She recognized him right off, having shot him once already. He walked around the side of the car while another man appeared in the headlights.

Shit, she thought. She couldn't rush the car with two more men shooting back at her. It was too risky.

The second man was bigger. He had dark skin and long black hair.

She stifled a gasp. Cole Tyler?

Angie leaned closer to the gap in the door, and cupped her right ear to listen. She could hear them speaking, but couldn't make out their words. Tyler stood near the front right headlight. He had his hands in his pockets as he looked across the houses.

Her gut twisted. She knew he couldn't be playing straight with her, but she never expected to see him here.

Hess had to have called him. There could be no other explanation. Could this whole ambush have been Tyler's idea? Just how far back did their relationship go, and what could be so important that he'd fly in from Minnesota to handle it in person? When this was all done, she'd have a lot of questions for him for sure.

"Hop in, we'll take you over there," the driver said. The man with the shotgun climbed in behind the driver, and Cole moved around to the opposite side.

Angie hefted the shotgun. She could end it all right now. Maybe get the car and arrest Tyler in the process.

The spotlight winked out and the car sped off down the street. Angie opened the door and stepped out onto the stoop. The car took a left two blocks down and disappeared.

"Shit."

THIRTEEN

SEAN COULD HAVE TOLD MOM the conversation with Ronnie wouldn't go well. He promised to talk to Ronnie for her, though he had no idea what to say to him.

Hey, sorry Mom and big bro kept you out of the loop. You cool?

Yeah. Not going to cut it.

He checked the garage first, thinking maybe his brother went to tinker with his motorcycle, but he found it locked tight and the lights off. Ronnie's truck was still parked out back, so he hadn't gone into town. No luck at Ronnie's cabin, nor at the house. If he shifted and went for a run, he could be anywhere.

Sean hoped Ronnie hadn't decided to take his frustrations out on campers again. They didn't need that kind of headache right now, and this time Mom just might kill him. Ever since Will died, Mom had been a lot more tense. On edge. Ronnie didn't take it much better, but the chip on his shoulder only made things worse.

They could all use some chill time. He got to vent his frustrations in the gym, but Mom, Cole and Ronnie lived and breathed the lodge. They buried their stress beneath more stress, and it was bound to blow up in their faces.

Enter the detonator, Agent Wallace. Saving her life had been the right move, no doubt. Now she had a job to do. Should they expect any less? Sean thought they should let things play out before jumping in and making things worse, but Cole wasn't happy unless he had some crisis to solve. Mom said he was like Dad that way.

Shit, that's it, he thought. Maybe Ronnie went to talk to Dad.

Sean returned to the house and went around to the backyard. He stepped into the woods behind the house and walked in a line straight out from the back door. A row of trees and a private drive separated the Tyler home from the field outside the main lodge building, and all of the campground maps clearly marked the house and surrounds as private. No trail or path led the way to the hollow a quarter mile out, and it didn't appear on any of the visitors maps, but Sean visited enough times over the years he could find it with his eyes closed.

He found Ronnie sitting on the small stone bench in the hollow, with a near-empty bottle of tequila at his side.

"Hey, man," Sean said. "How're you doing?"

"What do you suppose the old man would think?" Ronnie didn't turn around. He leaned forward, his hands clasped between his knees, and stared at the two wooden markers beneath the big tree fifteen feet in front of him. Ronnie had brought along a small kerosene camp lantern, and it cast a soft light across the markers' faces. The one on the left lost its luster to weather and time. The one on the right, not quite two years old, looked shiny and new in contrast.

"About what?"

"Anything! Everything! Take your pick!"

Sean sat down beside his brother. The bottle sat on the bench between them. Sean picked up the bottle, swirled the remainder around the bottom. Took a swig. At least Ronnie had picked the good stuff. He set the bottle down on his left side, away from Ronnie.

"Nice try." Ronnie held out his hand. Sean gave the bottle back, and Ronnie took a long gulp. "So?"

Sean shrugged. "I dunno, man. I wasn't even five when he died."

"You telling me you don't remember him?"

Sean winced at the disgust in his brother's voice. "Of course I remember him. But it's . . . little things. Mostly sitting in bed with him those last few weeks, listening to him read to me. Then he'd start coughing, and it scared the hell out of me."

"Mm." Ronnie seemed to ponder that a moment. "That shit wasn't right. Wasn't right at all."

Did he mean the memory or the cancer? Sean wondered. He decided to let it go.

"I assume this is about Cole?"

Ronnie harrumphed. "You know he's in Nevada?"

"Yeah."

"Figures. Mom doesn't keep secrets from you."

"Come on, it's not like that."

"Oh no? Did you know before or after he left?"

Sean weighed his response a moment too long.

"There you go," Ronnie said. "It is 'like that.' "

"She just didn't want you to do anything . . ."

"Stupid? Crazy?"

"Rash."

"Whatever." Ronnie snorted. "He's off to clean up a mess he created, but I'm the asshole."

"C'mon, do you really think Cole can't handle it?"

"I don't know what to think about Cole anymore! He's getting soft. If Dad were still alive, no way he'd have saved that fed. She'd be another name on a memorial and we'd be doing just fine."

"You could have taken care of that too, you know."

"You saying it's my fault now?"

"No, just calling you on your own bullshit. We all had a part in that night. You can't say what Dad may or may not have done differently."

"Like hell I can't."

"Then maybe you remember him differently than Mom and Cole do."

"Fuck you! Is that why you came out here? To tell me our big brother walks on water?"

"Nah, man. I just think he's doing what he thinks is right for the family, that's all."

"Now you sound like Mom. What about what we think is right? You can't tell me you're cool with him not letting you fight!"

Sean frowned. "That's different."

"Is it?"

"It's not that simple. They do blood tests and physical exams on fighters. If I get knocked out or blow out a knee, there would be CAT scans and MRIs. We don't know what they'd find in all that."

"Who are you trying to convince, me or you?"

Sean shook his head.

"We don't want anybody knowing what we are, fine," Ronnie said, "but I'm sick of hiding from our own shadows. At what point are our lives our own?" He stood and hurled the tequila bottle into the trees. It crashed through leaves and branches, struck a tree trunk with a thud. Then he kicked his boots off and stripped off his jacket.

"What are you going to do?" Sean asked.

"I'm going for a run."

"Do you think that's a good idea right now?"

"I don't know. Maybe I should call Cole and ask him."

"Seriously, you should come back to the house." Sean grabbed Ronnie's arm.

Ronnie ripped his arm free, his face twisted with rage.

Sean saw the punch coming. He took a half step back and let it swish past his face. He redirected the second punch with a simple palm block, then followed through and twisted Ronnie's wrist around and put him into an arm lock.

"Let go of me, asshole!" Ronnie shouted. The pain put him down on one knee, and he couldn't reach to punch Sean.

"You're drunk, Ronnie. Calm down."

"I am calm!"

"No, you're not. Stop fighting me and it will hurt a lot less."

"Goddamn it, let go!"

Sean applied more pressure to the arm lock, and Ronnie cried out. If Sean pushed much harder, he would dislocate his brother's shoulder.

"I can hold you here all night. Don't think I won't."

Ronnie twisted hard to his left and right for several more seconds, then relaxed at last. His breath came in great, heaving gasps.

"You done?" Sean asked.

"Yeah."

Sean released his arm and moved away. Ronnie stood, worked his shoulder. He clenched his fists.

"Knock it off," Sean said. "You're in no condition to fight."

"You're just like the rest of 'em. Go ahead, tell me it's my fault! Tell me Cole's cleaning up my mess!"

"Your fault? What the hell are you talking about?"

"Never mind." Ronnie turned and walked away.

Sean thought about stopping him, about grabbing him again, but instead watched him disappear into the darkness between the trees. Maybe it would be best to let him sleep it off, then talk about it when he could think straight.

Sean picked up the lantern and walked over to the wooden markers. He crouched in front of the old one and ran his fingers across his father's name carved into the face. Just what would Dad think of all this?

He looked over at Will's marker, cracked a sad smile.

"You tried, didn't you little brother?"

He stood, doused the lantern, and walked back to the house.

FOURTEEN

RONNIE FELT THE FURY building with every step. His
shoulders hunched forward, and his claws erupted from
his fingertips. The joints in his legs straightened, popped.
He stumbled into a tree and hit the ground. The cold,
damp earth soothed the heat surging through him. The
trees and brush closed in around him. He tore his shirt
off his chest, ripped open his jeans and stripped them
off.

He raked his claws through the mud. The heady scents
of the dirt and clay and decaying leaves filled his nostrils.
He rolled in it, dragged his body through it, smearing it
across his flesh and through the dark fur erupting in
scattered patches on his back, arms and legs. The
popping of his joints and crackle of his flesh and muscle
drowned out the winds whispering through the trees.

The world swam around him. He rolled up against the tree, pressed himself against the rough bark. His body heaved and spasmed. His tongue lolled out of his mouth and his breath came in great gulps and expelled itself in long bursts. His limbs pulled in tight, then stiffened and straightened in front of him. More fur filled in the gaps.

The wolf righted himself. Shook off the damp. He bared his teeth, growled deep in his chest as he sniffed the air. Then he cast his snout skyward and unleashed a long, deep howl.

He sprinted through the forest. His steps felt heavy, plodding, but he had no desire for stealth. The world parted around him, trembled at his passing, fled in his wake. He ran headlong across the hillside and down into the valley, down to the salt lick where the deer gathered.

The wolf burst into the field, kept on running. The doe's head snapped up and around, saw death bearing down on her. She jumped and ran, bouncing and leaping to shake off the hungry predator.

This wolf did not waiver. He knew the patterns of flight and the drives of instinct and fear, and he closed the distance as the deer tried to scramble up the hill into the shelter of the trees. He nipped at her tail and haunches, barking and snarling all the way, matching her step for step. He could smell the terror on her. He relished it. His hunger swelled.

At last he pounced. His claws found purchase in her back and her sides. His jaws clamped down around her neck. The sweet, hot taste of blood flooded his mouth as his weight drove the doe to the ground. She squealed and bucked as he bit the side of her neck and held her firm. Blood sprayed his face and fur. He chewed and shook her, dragged her down the hill. Felt her heartbeat fade with every passing second.

The doe went still, her breathing went shallow. The wolf jumped over her, bit into the soft flesh of her belly. Ripped and tore and pulled. He threw the ragged pieces all around and buried his snout deep in her guts. He gulped down flesh and muscle, chewed through bone and marrow. He clawed at her insides, shredding and tearing and pulling.

He rolled in the remains, reveled in the reek of blood and mud and shit. Went at the body with vigor and buried his head deep. He found her still heart, clamped his teeth around it and pulled, pulled, pulled until it tore loose with a wet and satisfying tearing of flesh. He chewed and chewed, bit it in half, gulped down the pieces.

At last he stepped back, sat on his haunches. His belly felt full and hot. Blood and flesh caked his fur so thick it crackled with his every breath. He shook it off like a wet dog, spraying it all around. He listened to it spatter the trees and the ground like rain.

Then he reared his head back and howled long and loud, and let the sound echo across the hills.

FIFTEEN

"WHY DOES EVERYONE CALL HIM SLICK?"

"It's a nickname," Lee grunted. "Same as we call you Cookie."

"Well, yeah, but mine's obvious." Bobby gestured at the vials and packets on the table in front of them. "How'd he get his?"

Lee frowned. His bushy, handlebar mustache curved down around it. "You telling me you've never heard this story?"

"Nope."

Lee turned. Bobby followed his gaze to Slick, a.k.a. Kelton Soames, lounging on a beat-up La-Z-Boy near the door. He worked his knife up and down a sharpener, and if he overheard Lee and Bobby talking about him, he didn't care.

"He got it in the joint. He worked up a knife out of angle iron or some such in the shop, smuggled it out, and slashed open a couple beaners in the showers. Blood just everywhere. The warden came down to check it out, slipped in the blood in his precious little wingtips and nearly went down on his ass. One of the bulls said 'Careful, it's slick,' and the name stuck."

"No shit. What happened to the guys he cut?"

"One's in the ground, the other will be shittin' in a bag the rest of his natural life. They put Slick in the hole for a while, but they never could pin it on him because nobody talked. You know how it is."

"Yeah," Bobby said. Actually he didn't. Closest he came was a short stint in a county lockup for possession. It could have been a lot worse if the prosecution hadn't dropped the intent to distribute charges, though. He had a box of his homebrew special, a stimulant cocktail he called Spanish Superfly, but nobody could properly identify it as a controlled narcotic, and they tried to con him into a plea deal. Instead, he ate the lesser charge.

When he got out, the university bounced him on ethics violations and declared his scholarship forfeit. The chem department chair told him no pharma company would ever even look at his résumé now, but that was cool; Uncle Evan hooked him up with the Swords, and he hasn't looked back.

It still felt odd being the focus of all this attention. Sure, Leland ran the shop and Uncle Evan was in charge, but the whole gig focused on his cooking up the stuff the

Swords shipped in. Cooking it into the meth was easy enough. Bobby just followed the directions, and the other guys handled all the heavy lifting. Truth be told, with a little instruction, Leland and Uncle Evan could handle it themselves. The Swords made it foolproof, delivering quality meth and ensuring he had good equipment that wouldn't blow up in his face. The wood shop's filters and blowers, not to mention all the paints, glues, solvents, and sealers, helped keep it all hidden from the authorities. A class A operation from top to bottom.

Hell, the Swords even taught Bobby to ride a motorcycle! He remembered riding down the block on Uncle Evan's Harley once or twice as a kid, but never thought he'd get his own Sportster. Evan said if he was going to work with the Swords, he might as well look the part. If he did his job right, he'd get his own back patch and rocker by year's end.

Way, way cool.

Leland took off his safety goggles and wiped the sweat off his brow with the fringe of his work shirt. Bobby winced and wondered if he shouldn't warn the older man about the potential danger of that, but thought better of it. Yeah, the guys knew he was important, but they tended to prefer he keep his mouth shut until he earned his keep.

Leland wasn't so bad. He was gruff, sure, but at least he didn't push Bobby around. He still wore his Chicago rocker with his colors when he rode, and he was a wizard with a lathe and a chunk of wood. He honed those skills while serving eight years for manslaughter. Bobby never did hear whom he killed, but he knew Leland recruited Slick into the club while inside.

Now he wondered if the incident where Slick got his name had anything to do with it. It sounded something like an initiation. He wasn't about to ask, though.

A few more minutes of tidying up and the shop was back to looking like any other wood shop. Clever repacking camouflaged the drug components amongst the shop's supplies and paints. They stashed the glassware and cooking equipment beneath the false bottoms in the shop's workbenches. It took Bobby three days to figure out the mechanism without Leland's help. As long as they scrubbed and bleached it all good, and the finished product went straight to the street or into one of Uncle Evan's stashes, there was nothing down there for dogs to smell.

Even the chem lab at the school didn't have gear this cool. Whoever shipped and prepped this stuff to them knew their job. Bobby felt if he did well here, then maybe he'd get called up to the big leagues and learn from the real pros. That's why he didn't dare sample any of this stuff; if he couldn't function, he could mess up huge.

That and he didn't dare experiment on himself. Spanish Superfly had nothing on the Swords' drug. Sure, it had a meth-like component for kick, but he didn't recognize the real payload. Most of the components came labeled in codes and batch numbers, and they changed from time to time. One of the couriers called it "Chimera" once, but Uncle Evan said they'd come up with something better for the street. Something flashier. Bobby suspected an artificial neurotransmitter or hormone in one batch, possibly affecting the amygdala based on the occasional bouts of fear and paranoia a couple of users complained about. One shooter reported a case of something like night terrors.

He didn't dare try to send anything out for an independent analysis, either. There's no way he could ever explain where he found it, and the Swords would kill him if it jeopardized anything they wanted to accomplish. Better to be patient and bide his time than to take Slick's knife in his ribs.

The shop door swung open and Evan pushed his way in.

"Someone want to tell me why there's blood in the parking lot?"

"That was my fault." Slick stood and slid his knife into his pocket. "A couple of buyers came around looking to score."

"The assholes from across the street?"

"Nah, just some laborers from the shop up the way. They won't be back."

"They shouldn't have been here at all!" Evan snapped.

"It was only a matter of time, Evan," Lee said. "They see us in our colors, they see us at the shop . . . even a junkie can put two and two together."

"We can't afford to get careless. Not now. The sooner we show this stuff works in this miserable shithole, the sooner we can move on. Minneapolis, back to Chicago, it doesn't matter to me."

"Come on, Evan, look around." Lee made a sweeping gesture across the shop. "There's a lot of money here, from the shop equipment to the cooking gear and the methods to hide it. If they just wanted to test a drug, they'd be sending us finished product to sell, not set up manufacture."

"Doesn't matter where it's made if we can nail down distribution. If we can put together a reserve before Sturgis, some of our brothers can take it home, start creating some demand."

"Is that what the Council wants?"

"Fuck the Council. We're going to show some initiative."

Lee shared a sidelong glance with Bobby, then shrugged. "It's your ass."

"Damn right it is, and I'm done sitting on it. Now finish up so we can get the hell out of here for the night."

"Suits me!" Slick said. "If we hurry, we can still make it to the bar and pick up some backwoods pussy!"

That didn't sound bad to Bobby. Maybe he could tag along. It had been a while, since Fall at least. He crouched down to finish securing the concealed latches, and heard a peculiar whine in the distance. It got louder with every second.

"Does anyone else hear sirens?" Bobby asked.

SIXTEEN

"NO MORE PISSING AROUND. We kill the bitch."
Hess's breath stank of cigar smoke and bad coffee.

"I need to find out why she's here," Cole said.

"Not from her you don't. She killed two of my men and
I'll be damned if I let her kill any more. Is that going to
be a problem for you?"

Cole balled his fists. Harvey and two more of Hess's
men stood in a loose circle around them. The chubby
guy to the right licked sweat from his upper lip. It wasn't
that hot out.

"No," Cole said. "I suppose not."

Hess's eyes narrowed. Seconds passed. Something
scuttled across the dirt behind Cole's foot. He fought
back the urge to shove Hess away. He wondered what
Chubby would do about it, or if Chubby would even be

fast enough to do anything about it. Harvey, though . . . he and his shotgun may be a problem.

At last the sheriff grunted and turned away. Chubby's shoulders sagged, and he let out a deep breath. Hess must be reaching deep into his bench to put a guy like this on the field.

"You ask me, she's out here on her own," Hess said. "She didn't identify herself to anyone, she's got no partner, and there's been no cooperation through normal channels. So I'll ask you again, Tyler, what the hell happened in Minnesota to make her come out here digging up bodies?"

"Kate's father."

"Who the hell is Kate?"

"The girl you gunned down with my brother."

Hess harrumphed. He pulled a cigar out of his breast pocket, snipped the end. He bit down on it and rolled it between his teeth for a moment.

"So there it is," he said. "She smells cover up but she doesn't have enough to open an investigation, so she comes down on her own to see what she can stir up."

"I could have told you that much," Cole said. "I still want to know why she's here. What she's looking for."

"You're missing the big picture, Tyler. She didn't know the first thing about me before she got here, or there'd be a whole flock of feds hauling me away in chains. She's not looking to solve a crime, or to seek justice for two young kids. This is all about you and your hairy alter-ego."

"What's your point? This is all my problem now?"

"No, we'll take care of this. Like it or not, we're partners and we'll swing together if she gets out of here alive. So, if it's all the same to you, I'd appreciate a little more fucking cooperation! I can't cover for you if you don't keep me in the loop!"

"Fine. Can we get on with it?"

Hess snorted. "You're welcome, you son of a bitch. We've switched the radios to channel three. She's got one, too, so don't use it unless you have to. We're going to drop you at the end of Third and let you work back toward Main."

Cole and Harvey climbed back into the cruiser. Cole wondered if he shouldn't have just stayed home, let Hess and his men make Wallace disappear. Even Ronnie would have approved of that plan. No more blood on his own hands, no paper trail of plane tickets. Let Hess deal with the blowback when the feds come looking for their agent.

If only it were that easy. If it came down to it, Cole had no doubt Hess would sell him out. No matter how Hess spun it, it would put Cole—and probably the rest of the family—right back in the Bureau's crosshairs for all those deaths at the lodge. If Hess had any physical evidence or photos to compare to the bodies from the lodge, then Cole would be the only link between the two events, no matter how incredulous a story about werewolves might sound.

After Will and Kate were murdered, Cole let Hess live because he needed him. A sheriff's death would have brought a whole lot of heat down on Sunset and in turn, down on Cole. He needed Hess to help cover it up, wrap it all nice and neat so the state police, the feds, or anybody else would have no reason to come digging up the bodies.

That left Hess with all the answers. Kill Hess, he would have Wallace and the Bureau to deal with, and hope Hess didn't have evidence stashed away somewhere. Kill Wallace, the Bureau comes looking for her. Kill them both?

Not an easy decision. He had hoped he could talk his way out of this. Steer Wallace away from Sunset and solve this without shedding blood. Too late for that now.

Maybe he should have stayed home and let Wallace and Hess sort it out after all. Sure, Hess would have killed Wallace, but there wouldn't be a plane ticket tying Cole to Sunset. He already saved her ass out in the snow back home, why should he have to do it again?

Because she's one of the good guys.

Because she fell into this mess, just like Will and Kate.

Because if he'd killed Hess two years ago, these men wouldn't be hunting her like a dog.

Well done, Cole, he thought.

The driver dropped them off at a dead end near the face of the rock wall. A dilapidated playground surrounded an aging Joshua tree. The jungle gym looked like the skeleton of some great beast that sought shelter beneath the tree as it died. Sand and dirt deposited by the dry desert wind piled up against the sides and fronts of the nearby houses.

Cole crouched down and picked up a handful of dirt, let it trickle back to the ground. He sniffed the air. If Wallace ran this far, it would only be to hide. She'd find no food here. No water and no way out. If they found her in one of these houses, she'd fight like a cornered animal.

"Well? What do you think?" Harvey put his shotgun across his shoulders and used it to stretch.

Cole looked over the houses. He pointed at a wide house on the corner, the only one on the block with a second story.

"Let's start there."

They walked soft to avoid loud footfalls on the long wooden porch as best they could. Harvey tried the front door handle, shook his head. The window beside Cole had been left open a couple inches. He eased his fingers through and lifted. They both winced at the horrendous noise of wood scraping on wood.

"Doesn't matter now, does it?" Cole opened the window the rest of the way and stepped through. Dust flew up at his passage, and he rubbed his nose with the back of his arm to prevent a sneeze. The interior might have looked nice once, but now dust covered everything. The thin carpet felt dry and crunchy beneath his boots as he went over and unlocked the front door.

"Smooth," Harvey said. "Real smooth."

"Shh! You hear that?" Cole looked up the stairs, craned his neck to try to see around the landing.

Harvey raised his shotgun. "What is it?"

"A footstep. Maybe a door."

"Go ahead, I'll cover you."

"No way, you've got the shotgun." Cole stepped back.

Harvey hesitated, chewed his lip.

"What's the matter?" Cole asked. "Afraid she'll shoot you again?"

"Bite me." Harvey leaned onto the step, tested it for his weight, then took the next step. He braced the shotgun against his shoulder and sighted down the barrel as he ascended. He almost looked like a pro.

Cole followed Harvey four steps up, then grabbed his ankles and yanked his legs out from under him. Harvey pitched forward and struck the steps face first with a yelp and a loud whack. Cole jumped up on Harvey's back and pinned him to the stairs with his knee. Harvey tried to push himself up, but Cole leaned his weight forward, then reached down and grabbed the shotgun with both hands, one on either side of Harvey's head. Then he pulled back hard, yanking the barrel tight across Harvey's neck.

Harvey gasped for breath. Something went crunch in his throat, and his legs flailed against the stairs. He tried to push the shotgun away but couldn't get any leverage. He tried to push up from the stairs and twist away, but the weight of Cole's knee braced against his spine pinned him in place. His breaths came in sputtering gasps. Cole pulled back harder, then harder still, at the same time leaning into his knee. Harvey's struggles weakened. He clawed at Cole's hands. One nail gouged the top of Cole's ring finger, drew blood. Cole ignored it, kept on pulling.

Harvey's struggles faded.

Faded . . .

Stopped.

Cole held on for a few seconds more, then loosened his grip. When Harvey didn't react, Cole stood and pulled the shotgun out from under the deputy's body. He walked down to the bottom step and sat down. The shotgun rested on his knees. His arms ached from the strain.

He turned the shotgun over in his hands. It felt heavy, lots of metal and plastic. Plenty of smooth surfaces for his fingerprints.

Worry about that later, he thought. He pumped it over and over, ejecting every round onto the floor. He stood and swept them with his foot, scattering them throughout the next room, then turned and pitched the shotgun the other direction.

Harvey's radio crackled. "Church Street's clear. Moving on."

Cole didn't recognize the voice. How many more men had Hess brought in? Best get a move on if he wanted to find Wallace first.

He took off his boots and socks and set them behind the door. He stripped off the rest of his clothes, bundled them up and wrapped them in his jacket, and set the whole package on his boots. The threadbare carpeting felt stiff and dry beneath his feet as he walked to the center of the front room.

He closed his eyes and fixed an image of Angie Wallace in his head. Dark, shoulder-length hair with a hint of red. Wide, bright brown eyes. Short, not quite to his chin, but strong. Athletic, like a runner, or a dancer.

His heart raced. His muscles tensed, then burned. A pricking sensation erupted all across his flesh.

He thought of her scent. Not just the cheap hotel shampoo he detected on the car seat, but her. Soft. Sweet. More he didn't have words for.

His jaw popped. His joints crackled and his bones shifted. Fur erupted across his arms, down his back, along his legs.

He hung onto that image, that scent. He remembered her in her hospital bed, in the lodge. The scent of her blood, hot and sticky in his fur, as he carried her through the woods.

His fingers and toes curled into claws. His jaw pushed outward, his teeth pushed through his gums. His ears shifted higher, turned forward. His heart pounded. His blood burned. Waves of pain rippled through his body.

Wallace's name was a dim echo in the back of his mind. He held tight to her face, to her scent. He remembered the sheriff's scowl and the scent of his cigars. He remembered his men in the desert with their guns.

The cool desert breeze whispered through his fur as he left the house.

Now the beast would hunt.

SEVENTEEN

"POLICE! SHOW US YOUR HANDS!"

Cops waving pistols and shotguns flooded into the shop from all sides. Some wore local or county uniforms; some wore street clothes. All meant business.

Evan tugged down his respirator and held up his hands. "Whoa, whoa! What's all this?" He shouted to be heard over the commotion, and over the shop's four large blowers, all running at full speed.

Leland leaned his mop against the wall and got down on his knees, then laced his fingers behind his head. He knew the routine.

Slick smirked behind his mask as three cops shouted at him and pointed guns at him. An officer made a grab for his wrist and he pulled it away. One cop kicked the back of his legs and dropped him to his knees, then two men tackled him to the ground. He grunted and strained as they held him down and wrestled his arms behind his back.

Bobby went straight to the ground, spread-eagled. A cop covered him with a 9 mm handgun pointed directly at his forehead. He fought a sudden urge to piss.

"Turn off the blowers!" a burly cop shouted at Evan.

"What?" Evan hooked his ear toward the cop.

"I said turn off the fucking blowers!"

"No way, man! The fumes are too dangerous!" He pointed at the huge pools of stain and sealer he and Lee had dumped all over the floor and one workbench not thirty seconds ago.

"You've got three seconds, asshole! One!"

"You want me to quote OSHA regs at you? Show you MSDSes? That shit's dangerous! Why do you think we wear these?" He shook his respirator at the cop. "And don't even think about firing those guns in here! You might spark up a nice fireball."

The cop popped him square in the nose with a strong left jab. Another officer wrenched Evan's arms behind his back and zip-tied his wrists together. He sniffed at the small trickle of blood in his left nostril as they put him on his knees.

The moment they had the four Swords rounded up and ensured the rest of the place was clear, they started rummaging through shelves and toolboxes. They threw boxes of screws on the floor and knocked over lumber. An officer tore open a trash bag of sawdust and poured it out on the floor. Another scattered the scrap wood pile. They shined flashlights into every dark corner, reached into every nook and cranny.

Then they brought in the dogs. Evan felt confident the shop setup would foil them well enough, and he hoped the fumes from the spill would confuse the dogs' sniffers.

He'd know in a few minutes.

"You boys got a warrant for all this?" he asked.

The cop pulled a folded sheaf of paper out of his back pocket and dropped it at Evan's feet. "Who's got the knife?"

"Knife? Man, we got knives and tools all over the place."

"The knife used in the fight outside."

"Are you kidding? That's what you're here for? Those guys were trying to rob us!"

"You don't seem to understand this has been a long time coming. That little stunt just sealed the deal."

Evan frowned. So somebody did call it in. Couldn't be the junkies Slick chased off. What would they say? They went looking to score some dope and got in a fight with a dealer? No, there had to be another witness.

The guys across the street. Had to be. The landlord's son watched them like a hawk. Fucker's probably been waiting for an excuse.

"What are you men still doing here so late?"

"Deadlines, man. See those two tables? They should have been delivered last week. Business has been too good and we're falling behind."

One of the dogs moved toward the workbench. It whined and snarled as its handler coaxed it on. It hesitated at one point, but turned a lap around the workbench before moving on to the next one.

Evan stifled a grin.

"So what's up?" he asked the cop. "You need anything? Chairs? Maybe a nice new gun rack?"

The cop glared. "You trying to bribe me?"

Evan laughed. "No way. I'll charge you, man. Just saying my men have skills. We can make you up something nice!"

"How about a dildo for your wife?" Slick asked. "I can make a big one, something she'll feel for a change!"

The other Swords laughed. A nearby officer kicked Slick in the ribs with the toe of his boot.

"That's brutality, man!" Evan said.

"Shut the fuck up. Save your breath for your lawyer when we find that shit you've been slinging around town."

Evan smiled. Good luck, pig.

EIGHTEEN

ANGIE PISSED IN THE DRY TOILET, then dabbed herself dry with the fringe of her jacket. She tried to flush out of habit, and shook her head.

What she wouldn't give for a glass of cold water. Her mouth felt dry and parched after all the effort of the evening. If she didn't get out of the desert in the morning, the heat of the day could become a real problem.

Her stomach rumbled. Her body ached. She needed water, food and rest.

Patience, she told herself. She couldn't let her physical needs cloud her judgment. If she moved around too much and they caught her in the open, it could get bad fast. If she tried to bait them with gunshots, she'd have all of them coming down on her and she'd be outgunned.

She had to bide her time, find her opportunity, then strike.

This house seemed as good a place as any to hole up for a bit. She finally found the downtown area again, then dropped back a few blocks to this place. It gave her proximity to her disabled rental in case anyone came looking for her or it, and was far enough away from the scene of the fight that any search team coming this way should be spread out enough from backup that she'd have a shot at them. The two front windows had been boarded over, giving her some extra cover, and the interior arrangement made it easy for her to cover both the front door and a side door with relative ease.

She set the shotgun in the corner of the room and sat down on the floor. A twinge in her hip made her wince, and she stretched out her leg. She set the revolver on the floor next to her so it wouldn't dig into her back.

The radio stayed quiet. She flipped to the next channel, and waited. They had to know she took it, but she doubted they could communicate effectively without it. It took a lot of work to coordinate a search this big, and the longer it took them the sooner others would start getting nosey. Someone was bound to miss one of the two men she killed, too.

She flipped to another channel.

Tyler's presence still didn't make sense. Obviously, someone in town—probably the sheriff, or someone in his office—contacted him after she arrived. If he had enough pull to get them to kill her, did he really need to show up on his own? She couldn't see why. Likewise, if the sheriff set this all up, what reason did he have to contact Tyler in the first place? They must both have an equal stake, something they're worried the other may screw up.

She flipped to another channel.

The files on the Will Tyler and Kate Henrikssen murders didn't have a lot of information. Their bodies were found in crude graves near an old mine in Sunset. Both had been shot in the head, and their bodies wrapped in quicklime. That, at least, spoke to the murderer's incompetence, as quicklime actually did more to prevent decomposition than to accelerate it. It perhaps covered the stench, but nothing more.

She flipped to another channel.

The murders were pinned on Marcus Rice, a resident of Sunset. Marcus's own brother, Charles Rice, had also been murdered not long before Will and Kate. Marcus was blamed for his brother's death much later, and it only showed Charles had been killed in his home. There was no mention of method or motive, and the coroner's report was suspiciously absent.

She flipped to another channel.

Cole Tyler arrived in Sunset a week after his brother and would-be sister-in-law disappeared. Within two days, a bartender, a deputy, and Marcus Rice were all dead, with Marcus Rice being killed by the sheriff in a shootout. The cause of death of both the deputy and the bartender was reported as "knife or similar edged weapon." Again, full autopsies were missing from their files.

She flipped to another channel.

What role did Cole Tyler play those two days? If Marcus Rice killed Will Tyler and Kate Henrikssen and hid the bodies, why did he not do the same with his brother? A deputy had also been killed, and a local bartender, too. If Rice killed the deputy to avoid custody, then why had the bartender been killed? A witness? A frame-up?

And why were none of them shot like Will and Kate? Where was the ballistics data from their bodies, and where were the murder weapons? If Hess pulled the trigger on them, as the dispatcher claimed, then it made sense the evidence would all disappear.

She flipped to another channel.

So, why? Why would Hess kill a young couple on their way to Vegas for a quickie marriage?

These are some of the questions she came to Sunset to find answers for. She expected resistance, but nothing like this. It felt more and more like a greater conspiracy going on. She never found a tie between Rod Babineaux's Las Vegas alias and Sunset—or Minnesota, for that matter, beyond the lodge cabin rental—but running guns sounded reasonable. It's a hell of a motive for murder and cover-up, if they were about to get discovered.

She flipped to another channel.

She rested her head against the wall. If they won't talk when she gets out of here, she'll bring the Bureau down on their heads. They'll tear into the sheriff's records, maybe close down the lodge until they can investigate possible trafficking. It would only be a matter of time before one of them flipped on the other, and the truth would come out.

She flipped to another channel.

Her eyelids felt heavy. She shook herself awake. Hold it together, Ange.

She flipped to another channel.

Her eyes closed. Her fingers relaxed, and the radio slipped out of her grip and to the floor.

NINETEEN

THE WOMAN.

Focus on the woman. This place, so foreign with its dry and dusty scents and the dry rasp of wind and sand, yet so familiar with those scents now associated with the deaths of his brother and his almost-sister. The beast remembered the other wolves. Remembered the sheriff and his filthy cigars. Memories that raised the fur along his spine and filled his muscles with blood.

This place promised violence. His claws twitched and flexed. Soon.

The woman came first. He saved her once. Saved her from the bullet that would have ended her life. Saved her from the men with guns, men like the ones lurking around him now. Now he had to find the woman again.

He crept through the old homes. Their reek betrayed their age and abandonment. The dry and brittle walls threatened to collapse at his passage. Rodents scurried from his path and under the floors, while insects scuttled across the ceilings. Sometimes he smelled stale urine or dried feces, and sometimes the cloying scents of abandoned food and garbage.

No trace of the woman's scent. Not yet. There could be no mistaking it amongst all this desolation and ruin. He kept moving, tracking through the streets and alleyways and across the yards. Focus. Find her.

He crept up to a narrow stair. Froze. Sniffed.

Body odor. Tangy cologne or aftershave.

Men.

He listened to the house. Waited. Heard no footfalls or voices. He backtracked through the scent, swung his head left and right to find its edges. Its path led him to the next house, where he listened again. Then to the next house, and the next still.

Then he heard them.

Two voices through the broken window to his right.

"All clear," one said.

"Here, too."

Their voices echoed from the other side of the house. He crept to the window, listened.

"Only three more houses on this block."

"Think we'll find her?"

"Someone had better soon. May as well be us."

The voices came into the front room, approached the window.

"What do we do then?"

"We pin her down and call for backup. We don't need to be heroes."

"Call how? I don't even know where I am!"

"It's a good thing I've been checking the addresses then, isn't it?"

The beast tapped on the windowsill.

"What the–? Did you hear that?"

"Shh! Idiot!"

The beast tapped again: *tap-tap-tap*.

"Go check it out." Whispering.

"Hell no! You do it!"

A sigh. "Pussy."

Footfalls approached the window. The beast stood to one side, watched the hole in the glass. His muscles tensed. His ears flattened, and he raised his claws. Spittle dripped from the corners of his jaws. A rifle barrel appeared in the hole. The front sight snagged the tattered curtain and swept it aside.

The beast reached through the window and grabbed the man, his claws raking through cloth and flesh for grip. He pulled. The remains of the window shattered and sliced at the man's face and arms. He screamed as he arced through the air, then grunted when he hit the ground. The beast swiped its claws across his throat and the underside of his jaw. Hot blood spurted across the beast's other hand, which still gripped the front of the man's chest, claws into him like cleats on turf.

The second man shouted and opened fire. Bullets flew through the shattered window and smacked against the house next door, then punched through the window frame and the wall below it. One zipped past the beast's ear, and it released the slashed man and dove to the ground. It rolled, returned to its feet and ran for the front of the house.

The shooting stopped.

Silence.

Then, "Holy shit, Larry!"

Larry gurgled and sputtered.

"Help! I need help, goddamn it! Oh, God, Larry, I think he's dying!"

A hiss of white noise, then "DJ? What's happening? Where are you?" Hess's voice.

"They got Larry, man! You need to get over here! We're on . . . shit . . . Jefferson, I think?"

"Sit tight, DJ. We're on the way!"

"Roger that." A thump. "Oh shit, oh shit. Larry, you still with me? Hang in there, man! Help's coming!"

Larry didn't make a sound.

The beast crept onto the porch. The men had left the front door open. He pushed through, and one of the hinges squealed.

"Who's there?" The man's voice went high, full of fear and desperation.

The beast took two more steps. The floor creaked beneath his weight.

The man fired two shots. The muzzle flashes lit up the next room. The beast flattened its ears against the noise hammering through the house.

"Fuck this!" the man said. Running footsteps retreated through the house.

The beast gave chase. Its heavy footfalls shook the room and rattled the remaining windows. It negotiated its speed and weight through the next room, into the one beyond and toward a side door just slamming shut. He spotted the man running for the street, smelled his sweat ripe with adrenaline and terror.

The man's boots thudded across the asphalt. His breaths came in short gasps. He was a big man. Fat. Slow. He glanced over one shoulder, as the beast closed in on him. The man's eyes went wide. He spun, brought around his rifle.

The beast grabbed the barrel. The rifle boomed and bucked, but the shot went wide. The beast yanked the rifle out of the man's grip, then smashed the stock down on his head. The man collapsed to a heap at the beast's feet. The beast clubbed him again and again. Bone crunched and broke, then the butt broke off of the wooden stock and skittered toward the curb. The beast hit the man once more, then flung the rifle into a nearby yard.

The beast took three steps back from the mangled body. The heady scents of blood, meat and marrow mingled in his nose. He licked saliva from his chops.

No. The woman. Find the woman.

The beast turned away, concentrated on her scent. She was here. Close. He loped across the yards, sniffing, smelling.

Headlights appeared up the street. Distant, but coming fast. A second set joined them from an adjoining street.

The beast wanted to fight, but knew the men would have guns. He didn't want to be in the open. He could deal with them later. He had to find the woman first.

The beast ran between the houses and to the next block to resume the hunt.

TWENTY

HESS CROUCHED BESIDE THE MANGLED REMAINS of DJ Morris. The guy had wanted to be a deputy for the better part of seven or eight years, but Hess always found him too heavy around the waist, and too light in the nutsack. He was eager to please, though, and good at keeping his damned mouth shut. He had a certain malleability about him that made him useful for jobs like this.

Not so much anymore. Hess had seen car accident victims with less trauma than this.

"Are we sure she hasn't gotten a hold of a car?" Hess asked.

"Far as I know, they're all accounted for, Sir." Deputy Denton had the initiative of a desert tortoise, but the attitude of a sidewinder. He got booted from the Reno

PD for smacking around some tourists. That suited Hess's needs just fine.

"How about you get on the horn and find out?"

"Yes, Sir." Denton stepped away a few paces and spoke into his shoulder mic.

Hess didn't expect they'd find anything. If Wallace snagged a car, she was already gone. No, the body and the broken rifle suggested he had a much bigger problem now.

"Jerry! Over here!"

Tim McCabe shouted to him from a few houses up the street. Hess stood and trotted over, then shined his flashlight on McCabe. Sweat drenched his pale face.

"What is it?"

"We found Larry Hawkins."

McCabe stepped aside and Hess walked past him into the space between the two houses. He heard a retching sound and used his flashlight to find Gordy Lewis dry-heaving against the wall. He'd already painted the ground and his boots with the contents of his guts.

Hess shifted his flashlight a few yards over to illuminate the body on the ground. Larry Hawkins died with his eyes cast skyward, his mouth agape and flooded with blood, and his fingers buried in the ragged slashes in his throat. Larry had hunted with Hess many times in the past, both wild game and the occasional errant scumbag. Larry had even been there when the hunting group discovered the Rice brothers out in the desert some twenty years back.

Now Hess had one less hunting partner, and Sunset had lost its only butcher.

"Son of a bitch," Hess muttered. He gripped his flashlight in his armpit and pulled his pistol. He popped the magazine and slipped it into the corresponding holster in his belt, then reached for his back pocket and removed the magazine of his special loads. He slid the magazine home and racked the slide.

"Sheriff? Everything okay?" McCabe asked.

"Get back to the car," Hess said. "Now!" He braced the flashlight across his gun hand and swept it up and down the alley and across the houses, then made a quick sweep across the rooftops just to be sure.

McCabe and Lewis didn't argue. They took their cue from Hess and shouldered their rifles, watching in all directions as the three of them moved back toward the street. Lewis had a flashlight mounted to the underside of his shotgun, and he swung it in tandem with Hess's.

McCabe knew about the Rices, about what they could do. He'd never seen them change like Hess had, never saw the things they could become, but he knew well enough the secrets a select few in Sunset helped keep. It also explained the pants-shitting terror Hess saw in McCabe's eyes not thirty seconds ago.

Lewis didn't know shit. Sure, he had to have heard the stories and the rumors that circulated around town, but he seemed to maintain a policy of "I don't want to know nothin'." He had chopped and scrapped Will Tyler's car, and later gutted the blood-soaked interior of Deputy

Raines's cruiser, no questions asked. Plausible deniability, like he was some goddamn movie president.

As for Denton, he'd just have to learn the hard way. Hess brought him aboard for his moral flexibility and his kick-ass attitude, but there was a lot he hadn't shared with the new deputy yet. Hess felt he'd picked the right guy for the job and Denton would pull the trigger on a fed if directed, but facing down goddamn werewolves would challenge even the hardest of men.

First things first: they had to regroup and rethink their plan before they got torn apart.

Denton appeared on his left side, his Mossberg shouldered.

"What have we got?"

"We're pulling back," Hess said. "Get back to the car."

"Is she in there?" Denton asked. "I can—"

"Don't argue with me, goddamn it! Do it!"

"Yes, Sir." Strictly professional. The guy just may survive this.

They hustled to the cars in a group, their weapons fanned out in a broad pattern around them. The bodies would have to wait.

"Regroup on Main, near the woman's car. Stay sharp and shoot anything that doesn't identify itself."

"You don't have to tell me twice," McCabe said. He and Lewis climbed into the first car.

"You're driving." Hess tossed Denton the keys to his truck, then walked around to the passenger seat. They both climbed in and slammed their doors shut, and Denton followed Lewis down the street.

"What's this about, sheriff?" Denton asked.

"The situation has changed. Shut up and give me a few minutes to think."

TWENTY-ONE

NINA FOUND SEAN STANDING at the kitchen counter, wolfing down a six-egg omelet and a ham steak.

"Haven't we talked about eating the restaurant food?" she asked.

"It's cool, Ma. These were on the verge of expiring."

"Uh-huh." She poured herself a cup of coffee, then leaned against the counter beside him. "So where was your brother last night?"

Sean froze mid-chew, gave her a dopey look. "You mean Ronnie?"

"This isn't the time, Sean. He wasn't in his cabin this morning. Did you find him? Where was he?"

"I don't know."

She narrowed her eyes, cocking her head to one side.

"Oh, come on, Ma. Not the look."

"Where, Sean?"

"Seriously, I don't know."

She held her stare.

"What, you think he ran off to Nevada or something?"

"The thought crossed my mind."

"Come on, he wouldn't really do that."

She gave him another sidelong glance.

"Okay, maybe he would, but truth is, he went out for one of his runs last night."

Nina sipped her coffee. Waited a moment. "And?"

Sean shrugged. "That's it."

She took another sip of coffee, then swirled it around her mug a bit.

"Okay, okay. He might have been drinking."

"What!?"

"A little! I mean, I think."

"Sean, you better come clean with me right now."

Sean deflated. He dropped his fork on his plate and turned to face her. "I found him sitting out in dad's hollow. He had a bottle with him, we had a little argument, and he took off."

"Argument about what?"

"Ah, you know. The usual. It was all drunk talk."

"So he was drunk."

"No! Well . . . yeah. A little."

"Sean, if you say 'a little' one more time, I swear—"

"He wasn't that bad! I mean, it's not like we've got cops knocking on the door or panicked customers fleeing for their lives, right?" He grinned.

"Not funny."

"No, but you know what I mean."

Sean may not be worried, but it scared the shit out of Nina. Ronnie had been growing more and more resentful of his older brother since Will died. At first, she thought it would blow over, but it only got worse after the gunrunners came around. Maybe she should have included Ronnie from the beginning, but Cole had a better handle on things, a more mature outlook. The family couldn't afford to let instinct and emotion rule their actions, and Ronnie had that in spades.

When this blows over, they would all have to sit down and talk this out. Even better, get away for a while. Get away from the lodge and the stress, decompress, and work this all out. A family vacation, of sorts, where they could hash things out and unwind. Reconnect. Get past all this nonsense that drove them apart and move on.

"Have you heard from Cole at all?" Sean asked.

Nina's gut clenched. "Not since he landed."

"I'm sure he's fine."

If anybody can handle himself, Cole can.

But some reassurance of positive progress would be nice.

"Do you think I could shoot out to the club again this afternoon?" Sean asked.

"I don't know, things are a bit crazy right now."

"Yeah, I know, but I'd like to talk to Dustin about a few things."

"Sean, this really isn't the time for–"

"It's cool, Ma. I'm not going to do anything rash. I just want to ask him about my training and all."

Nina frowned. Sure, things were quiet at the lodge right now, but with Agent Wallace stirring up trouble, Ronnie all wound up, and Cole out of pocket, she didn't want to be spread too thin. Nor did she want the boys too far if Cole hit the panic button.

Then again, Sean needed to blow off steam his own way. The rest of the staff could fill his duties, and despite Ronnie's influence, Sean would follow Cole's lead.

"We've got three campsites vacating this morning. Can you spot-check them before you leave?"

"Sure, Ma. No prob."

"You'll keep your cell handy?"

"Absolutely." He drew a cross over his heart.

"Alright, then. Go ahead."

"Thanks, Ma. You rock." He leaned over and gave her a peck on the cheek.

"Just don't make me regret it."

"You know I won't."

No, he probably wouldn't.

But there have been many surprises lately.

TWENTY-TWO

RONNIE STOOD UNDER THE SHOWER, letting the hot water soothe his aching head. Blood sluiced from his body and swirled down the drain. After a few minutes, he scrubbed at the dried-on bits with a washrag. He combed more muck out of his hair with his fingers. One of these days, he thought, he just might have to cut it short like Sean's.

He wondered how things were going in Nevada. Had Cole checked in yet? Had Mom heard anything at all? He thought about calling Cole himself, but big brother had already made it clear that it was none of his business. Cole would handle it his own way, and once again the rest of them would be stuck dealing with the mess.

If Cole had handled it right the first time, it wouldn't matter what Lars Henrikssen told her about Nevada, or if they'd let the fed bitch die in the snow. If that sheriff were out of the picture, there'd be nothing left in Nevada for anyone to find.

Of course, Cole would counter none of it would have happened if Will and Kate hadn't eloped. If they hadn't stopped in that little shithole of a town or just stuck home near the family, they'd still be alive today.

Ronnie punched the wall. His fist struck tile over the stud and pain radiated down his wrist. Fuck it, he deserved it. He punched the wall again, and a crack appeared across the grout between the tile and the next one up.

If Ronnie hadn't encouraged Will to take Kate to Vegas, they'd still be alive. The sheriff would never have entered the picture, and this whole affair would have died with the smugglers and skinheads out on the range.

You couldn't have known, he told himself for the thousandth time. He couldn't predict Sheriff Hess would be out there waiting. The family didn't even know there were any human wolves like them out there, much less one with the stones to commit fratricide.

Fucking fate. Every family relationship seemed doomed to fail. When Will said he wanted to take Kate to Vegas, Ronnie couldn't agree fast enough. He never wanted them to die. They were so happy together, so full of love it damn near made the family sick. They didn't deserve to suffer the same fate as he and Julia Ramos back in high school.

Jesus, Julia . . . Ronnie hadn't thought of her in months. The accidental pregnancy, the abortion he pushed her to have.

The hatred she poured upon him afterward.

No. Will and Kate deserved better. It was better for them. Different. They could have beaten all that if some hick fucking sheriff hadn't put a bullet in their heads.

At least they had died together.

Ronnie laughed, but without humor. He deserved a bullet just thinking that way.

He didn't dare tell Cole. Big Brother would throw it right back in his face. Born not even two years earlier, and that makes him smarter than the rest of them? Better? Bullshit. If things kept going the way Cole led them, they'd have more feds than he could count crawling up their asses by sundown.

Hell, maybe they'd be better off that way. Draw them all out, finish them all at once. It worked well enough last winter, with one obvious exception. It felt right, too, like it was meant to be. Defending their territory, like they were made to do.

"That's right," he muttered. "Fuckin' made for it."

Outside the bathroom, the front door latch clacked open and the handle bumped against the inside wall.

Shit.

"Who's there?" he called.

"Oh! Housekeeping, sir, I'm sorry. I thought you had checked out."

"Amy?"

Stunned, uncertain silence.

"Just get in here," he said.

Amy appeared in the bathroom door, a swirly, mottled splash of color through the glass pattern in the shower stall door.

"Ronnie? What are you doing out here?"

"Takin' a shower. What's it look like?"

She chuckled. "No, butthead, I mean why in a rental instead of your place?"

"I was in the crawlspace working on the plumbing. As long as I was testing it, I figured I might as well get cleaned up."

In truth, he woke up in the forest with one hell of a headache and no idea where he'd left his clothes. He snagged a set of mechanic's coveralls and a spare key from the garage, then waited in the woods until the renters packed up and left. After waiting a few minutes to be sure they didn't come back, he came in and got into the shower.

"Do you need a fresh towel?" Amy asked. "I've got plenty in the car."

"Sure." It occurred to him, maybe its high time to correct his own fate. "Hey, close the front door when you come back in."

"You better not be thinking what I think you're thinking. I've got work to do!" Her voice trailed off as she walked away. A few moments later the front door closed, and her voice zoomed back in. "Here's your towel. I'm going to pick up and then get started on the beds."

"Wait." Ronnie slid the door open.

"Ronnie! You're getting water all over the floor!"

"The maid will clean it up."

She put her hands on her hips. "Ha-ha. Jerk."

"Take your clothes off."

"C'mon, I don't have time—"

"Sure you do. Take your clothes off."

"If I don't get a move on with these rooms, your mother is so going to fire me." Throughout her protests, she took off her jacket and pulled at her shirt.

"You let me worry about that."

She draped her shirt across the sink and went to work on her shoes. He watched as more of her flesh appeared, bit by bit. He followed the lines of her muscles and the curve of her hips, let his gaze linger on the swell of her breasts. Talk about made for it . . .

At last she stood nude before him, and struck a pose as if presenting herself.

"Ta-da!" she said. "Now what?"

"Get in here." He moved aside.

"What will I say when people notice my hair is wet?"

"Who's going to ask? Just tell them you had an accident in one of the cabins."

She put her hands on her hips. Then huffed a deep breath and stepped into the shower. She cringed as the water hit her.

"Yikes! You used up most of the hot water already. I think—"

He pulled her to him and pressed his mouth to hers. She relaxed against him, returned his kiss for a moment, then pulled her head back.

"What's gotten into you this morning?" she asked.

He kissed her again, then pulled her tight to him. His stiff penis pressed against her lower belly, and she let out a throaty chuckle.

"I guess that explains it," she said.

Ronnie grabbed her by the shoulders and turned her around, then bent her over. She braced herself against the wall as he lined himself up. He thrusted into her, and she let out a moan. He went at her fast and hard, pulling her hips against his. Their thighs slapped together, making the water splash. His feet slipped inch by inch across the tile and he braced his heels against the sides of the stall.

He thrust harder and harder, still hanging on to those wide hips, so perfect for bearing his children. He could see the muscles in her back tightening, the clench of her glutes and thighs, and knew they'd be strong children. Damn right he would reclaim his own fate.

Harder, faster. Her face, and then her shoulders, pressed against the shower wall. She grunted, whether in pain or pleasure, or both, he didn't stop. She grabbed the showerhead and tried to pull herself up, but he did not relent. Harder, deeper, until at last he felt himself building to a climax. One more deep plunge and he held it there, released his seed into her. Her hips shuddered in his grip as he held the connection.

"Oh, my." Amy sagged against the shower wall for a moment.

Ronnie ran a hand up her back and down her side. A boy, he decided. Someone to keep the bloodline going. A start to his own family.

His own pack.

Breathless, Amy stood and slid off of him. She rinsed the sweat from her face in the cool water, then leaned back against Ronnie. Her hand reached back, found his ass, squeezed.

Ronnie wrapped his arms around her and caressed her belly with his hands. He took in the smell of her, relished the feel of her supple flesh and the firm muscle beneath.

"Is that offer to crash at your place still good?" he asked.

TWENTY-THREE

"AGENT WALLACE."

Angie snapped awake with a gasp and snatched up the shotgun. She shouldered the weapon and swept it across the room.

Nobody.

The radio lay on the floor between her knees. Soft blue light filled the room. She must have fallen asleep, she realized, and dreamed the voice. She leaned her head back to the wall and rested the shotgun on her thighs. Stupid, stupid, stupid. Anybody could have come in and caught her completely—

"Agent Wallace."

She snapped the shotgun back up.

"Who's there?" She already knew the voice.

"It's Cole Tyler." His voice came from the door to her left, but she saw nothing but dust and cobwebs through the opening.

"Show yourself."

"Put your gun down and we'll talk."

"Not happening." It sounded like he stood on the right side of the door. She aimed the shotgun just outside the doorjamb, and just above the light switch. "You come out with your hands up and maybe I won't blow your goddamn head off."

She got her feet under her as she spoke, then pushed against the floor and slid her back up the wall. Her hip protested with a jolt of pain, and her ass ached from sitting on the floor all night.

"In time. I'm not armed, and if I wanted to hurt you, I would have attacked you in your sleep."

The thought crossed her mind. She stepped sideways toward the window, risked a glance outside. She didn't see anyone out front, nor did she see anyone through the window on the opposite side. She allowed the silence to draw out between them and used it to listen to the house. No footsteps, no rattle of weapons. Just a soft creak as Tyler shifted his weight in the next room.

"Agent Wallace?"

"Where are your friends?"

"They're not my friends. I took down three, but there are several more."

"Why, Tyler? Why did you come here?"

"To keep you out of trouble."

She let out a derisive laugh. "You're doing a fine job of that."

"I promise you, I'm on your side, here."

"Prove it. What's your connection to Hess? Who really killed Kate Henrikssen?"

"We don't have time for this now. Hess and his men are setting fires all over town to flush us out. We need to get moving."

Angie pursed her lips. Part of her wanted to shoot him and make a run for it. Her analytical self took her to the window. She scanned the houses up and down the street, then craned her neck to look over the rooftops. Three columns of dark smoke rose into the air, one of them just a block or two over.

"I killed three of Hess's men," Tyler said. "By now he's figured that out and they want both of us. We need to move."

"Then you'd better give me the abridged version!" she snapped. "We're not going anywhere until you give me some answers!"

Silence. Did he not want to talk, or was he putting together a new bullshit story? The shotgun drifted down as they spoke, and she corrected her aim. If he was just buying time to try something, she would put an end to it real quick.

"Hess killed Will and Kate," he said at last. "A man named Marcus Rice framed my brother for murders he committed, including his own brother. As you're already finding out, the good sheriff has his own way of dealing out justice. When I went looking for Will, I exposed Marcus, but not before he could kill two more people. I took him down, but it was Hess who put the final bullet in him."

Angie thought back to what little she knew about those deaths. The deputy, the bartender. The pieces fit, but they still didn't quite add up.

"What's your connection to Hess? You say the man killed your brother. Why not kill him then?"

He snorted. "Not a day goes by I don't ask myself the same thing. Truth be told, I needed him. All those deaths would have landed squarely on my head, otherwise."

Angie's arm ached from holding the shotgun. Her head throbbed. She needed food and water, and she had no desire to get cooked alive by the sheriff's flames. She wanted to believe Tyler. Badly. She could use some backup in all of this, but she couldn't let that cloud her judgment.

"Why?" she asked. "Why the cover up? Why get rid of the bodies? Why the vague paperwork?"

"The bodies were . . . mauled."

"'Mauled?' Mauled how?"

"You've seen it. It was just like the bodies of the skinheads and the gunrunners."

"How, Tyler!?"

Silence again. Then, "You're not going to believe it."

"Try me!"

"Marcus Rice and his brother were . . . werewolves."

"Jesus Christ, don't patronize me! You're going to have to do a lot better than that or I'm going to shoot you where you stand!"

"Think about it! How well do you remember the night you were shot? You saw the bodies. Your men, the police, they were all shot. But the bad guys? Animal bites. Ripped flesh. They were all torn apart, right?"

Angie's finger tensed over the trigger. Her whole arm tightened up and her teeth ground together. One quick squeeze and the bullshit ends, but damn it, she remembered the medical examiner's speculation on some of the wounds: large canine bites. They found no other weapons on the scene and no other survivors to offer a better explanation. She got shot before she saw anything.

"Hess knew about the Rice brothers all along," Tyler continued. "He carried silver bullets and I'm sure he's got a nasty scar on his shoulder to back it up. Why else would I want to keep my family out of it? Why else would I need him to cover it all up for us?"

Shoot him, she thought. Just fucking shoot him.

"I can prove it. Look, I'm unarmed."

His hands appeared in the doorway, open and empty. She dipped the shotgun to aim at them, took a step back. Dark smears covered his right hand and part of his arm.

"I'm coming out. Don't shoot."

"No promises."

He stepped into the doorway, naked as the day he was born. He held his hands out wide, palms out, displaying a long frame packed with muscle. More dark smears marred his face and chest. Strands of his long, black hair stuck to the muck.

"On your knees!" she shouted. "Now!"

He dropped down to one knee, then the other, his hands still held out wide.

"Is that blood?"

"I told you, I killed three of Hess's men."

"You're no monster. You're a lunatic!"

"I said I can prove it. Just remember, I'm on your side." He raised one hand, then winced as his fingers spread with a muted crackle.

His hand changed. His fingernails grew. Hair erupted down the backside of his arm. She watched him transform. Her jaw dropped, and with it, the shotgun eased toward the floor. She looked at the claws, then looked at the blood on his arm, on his face and neck.

"Stop it!" She took three rapid steps forward and aimed the shotgun directly at his face. "Stop it right now!"

"Okay! Look, it's still me! Calm down! Calm down." He gestured with his hands, both the normal one and those bloody claws. "I promise you, I'm on your side."

Angie's hands trembled. The connecting ring for the shotgun's shoulder strap rattled.

"My brothers and I saved you once, our way. Let me help you again."

"Why?" she demanded. "How do I know you won't turn on me the second this is over?"

"I'm on your side, Agent Wallace. I'm putting it all on the line here. We don't have time for debate or acceptance."

She couldn't argue that point. The house had grown darker, not lighter, and she smelled the smoke from the burning houses. Whatever Cole Tyler may be, he appeared to be on her side. Roll with it, take down Hess and his men and survive. Sort the mess later.

"You stay where I can see you at all times," she said. "You come at me, threaten me, or so much as startle me, I put you down. You hear me?"

"Fair enough."

Angie lowered the shotgun. "Then let's get the hell out of here. And for God's sake, put on some pants."

TWENTY-FOUR

"YOU MEN ARE OUT OF HERE. I just wanted to give you fair warning I'll be filing eviction proceedings this afternoon."

"Like hell!" Evan shouted. "We have a lease!"

"My lawyer says there are at least three clauses we can show you've broken. If you like, you can take it up with your lawyers."

Evan clenched his fists. His breath fumed. He tried to keep his cool, tried real hard, but every muscle in his body ached to choke the living shit out the landlord. The guy's kid watched from across the street though. Evan could see him over the man's shoulder, leaning against the wall, his arms crossed, trying to look casual and tough all at the same time. Evan didn't fear the confrontation, but he didn't want to give the cops another excuse to come back.

The pigs left empty-handed an hour ago, leaving Evan and his crew with one hell of a mess to clean up. The stashes and setup worked perfectly, though, and he didn't know where, when, or even if he'd ever be able to reproduce it, especially in Emington.

"I thought this was America," Evan said. "We're innocent until proven guilty. If the cops had anything on us, they'd have arrested us. Look here—no cuffs." He held up his wrists and banged them together.

"Can we be frank with each other?" the landlord asked.

Evan shrugged. "Absolutely."

"When you fellas moved in and I found out you were all part of a motorcycle club, I was willing to turn my head and see how things played out. I didn't want a stereotype to color my judgment, and for a while you were great tenants turning out a good product."

"Well there you go, you—"

"But! It's no secret what you've been up to. This may be a small town, but we're not ignorant. Maybe the police didn't find anything this time, but they will, and soon, and I'd just as soon not have valuable property destroyed in the process."

"You can't do this." Evan didn't know what else to say. He didn't know leases and law well enough to argue, and he couldn't well beat the man into changing his mind. At least not in broad daylight, anyway.

"I'm sorry, but it's already done. And I'll kindly remind you you'll get your security deposit back, assuming the property and premises are intact. Have a good day."

The landlord took a few steps back, turned, and walked away. Evan watched him go until he reached the street, then went back into the shop and slammed the door shut behind him. Cookie flinched and nearly dropped his mop.

"What's up?" Leland asked him.

"He's kicking us out."

"Shit . . . What do we do?"

"I don't know. Let me think a minute."

He wanted out of this town, but dropping the ball on such a small operation wouldn't endear him to the Swords leadership. If they wanted him working in Emington, then he damn well had to make it work or they'd strip him of his chapter and ship him back to Chicago. He'd lose the respect of his old crew and would be stuck doing bitch work until the law caught up with him or he caught a bullet.

If he was lucky.

In '03, a crew down in Miami flubbed a job. B&E and arson, the rumors went. They got picked up, including the chapter president, "Dagger" Morton. Some mysterious lawyer swooped in and sprung him, and they both promptly disappeared. The crew pleaded out with public defenders and did their time. Meanwhile, pieces of Dagger showed up in four states.

Message received.

Evan kicked a small can of wood stain. It arced through the air, struck the block wall, and clunked to the floor. The lid cracked open and a pool of Royal Mahogany oozed across the floor.

"Damn, Uncle E!" Cookie ran over and picked up the can. "I just mopped that spot!"

"Shut the fuck up."

"So what's our move, Boss?" Slick asked.

Evan watched Cookie smear the stain around with a mop. If they could head off the landlord before he filed the eviction papers, they just may have a shot at keeping the place. Unless, of course, the guy's kid had the power to do the same, in which case they would just delay the inevitable. No, they had to take them both out, and they had to make it look good.

He paced for a moment. What if the junkies the other night just had the wrong place?

"Call Sid, Tully and Nick. I want them here in half an hour, ready to rumble."

◆ ◆ ◆

Bobby didn't like this plan.

He wasn't naive. He knew there would always be danger in the drug trade, but this wasn't what he signed up for.

Not that he would dare tell Uncle Evan that. He nodded along with grim faces gathered around the table, said he understood, said he was ready to go, but all the while he wondered if the Swords' leadership would approve of this plan. If one little thing went wrong, it could leave the club exposed to a whole lot of shit.

Bobby thought of the Swords' emergency phone. Uncle Evan had only showed it to Bobby once. He kept it on a charger hidden behind a neon Budweiser sign in his garage. It looked like any other clunky old cell phone, with a stubby plastic antenna molded into the chassis and a square LCD screen. It had one phone number programmed into the contact list.

"This is for emergencies," Uncle Evan had said. "I'm talking dire emergencies, like I'm dead or something. I don't know who exactly is on the other end, but I know they'll take care of things."

This felt like a pretty big emergency, Bobby thought. He wanted to trust Uncle Evan, but this just didn't feel right.

Too late now, though. Things were moving too fast. The gang was ready to move.

If things *did* go sideways, well, then that's why they had the phone in the first place.

TWENTY-FIVE

HESS CHUCKED THE STUB OF HIS CIGAR off the rooftop and watched its amber glow arc through toward the street below. It struck the hood of Denton's patrol car with an explosion of orange embers, then bounced to the ground and disappeared on the other side of the car. His truck bumper butted right up to its rear end, and every other car they had lined up nose-to-tail down the center of the street behind it. The wreck of Wallace's car capped one side of the street, and all the keys laid in a pile a few feet away, easy to keep an eye on, yet easily accessed in an emergency.

His radio crackled to life. "All done, sheriff. Over."

"Good job, Lewis. Get back here and get in position."

"Copy that. We're on the way."

"That's all of 'em," Hess called to the others. "Stay sharp."

He had split the group into two teams, then placed one on each roof flanking the line of cars. If Wallace and Tyler wanted out, they either braved the baking desert with no food and water, or they showed up here.

The fires only rushed the inevitable. He surveyed the smoke rising up in a wide arc all around town. Most of the houses went up like tinder, and he could even see flames flickering across rooftops at several points. Ash rained down around the center of town, and the wind worked in their favor, pushing the flames in their direction.

The huge columns of smoke rose high into the air and would be visible for miles as the sun rose. A simple phone call ensured Sunset FD wouldn't respond, and with a few more calls he told two other possible responders he and his men were doing drills and fire practice and to hang back unless they were called. They agreed, but he hoped the quantity of smoke wouldn't prompt a response anyway. Nobody would really miss this town, but they wouldn't want out-of-control brush fires raging across the countryside, either. Hess didn't think the fires would spread far across the desert scrub, but it was a chance he was willing to take at the moment.

Just a few more hours . . .

Denton patrolled the far side of the roof. He'd upgraded from the department-issue shotgun to his personal scoped AR-15 from his trunk. The shotgun waited within easy reach, for emergencies. He kept his cool while the others went out starting fires, but he hadn't said much since Hess dropped the bomb on him.

Hess stepped up beside Denton, then spoke quietly so the others wouldn't overhear.

"How you holding up?"

"Good to go, Sir," Denton said.

"Don't give me that military bullshit. Speak your mind, son."

Denton pursed his lips. He seemed to weigh his words carefully. Hess liked that, though he would accept only one response.

"This isn't the right time for you guys to be screwing with me, but . . ."

"But it's a big pill to swallow."

"The biggest. How scared should I be?"

Hess spat over the roof's edge. "Kid, if you aren't downright terrified, I'd assume you were full of shit or dumb as dirt. Just know he can die, just like you and me. I put one down myself."

"What? How many of these things are there?"

"Today? Just one." His kin would be a matter to deal with later. "You put a bullet in him, it's done."

"This is only a .223. Is it going to be enough gun?"

"Whatever you see out there, remember there's still just a man in there. He's not a charging fucking rhinoceros. That's why I put us on these rooftops. He's got to get in close, like an animal. You find him in that scope, you don't give him the chance. Even if it doesn't kill him, if he's wounded we can get in close and finish the job."

Denton chewed his lower lip, nodded.

"As for myself," Hess said, "I'm more worried about the woman. She's the one with the guns . . . and the training."

"Roger that. Do these other guys have the stomach for this, Sir? I know Sam's good, but the rest strike me as a little green."

"They're not hard men, but they'll do the job. They know what's at stake."

"And that is?"

"Hard time. We've buried a lot of secrets in Sunset, and the things we've done the last twenty-four hours are just the beginning." Hess walked the few paces to the corner of the building and mulled that over for a moment. "By the way, son, I know this ain't your fight."

"You don't have to worry about me, Sir. You hired me and I aim to get the job done." He turned to face Hess, looked him dead in the eye. "I've also been busting heads for you long enough to know there's a lot of shit going down behind the scenes. I've been kinda hoping some of it's even been profitable."

Hess's eyes narrowed. Seconds passed, and the deputy did not flinch. Now it all made sense. The kid couldn't get a job elsewhere, and wouldn't go back to honest work. Laborer? Truck driver? No, this kid had a taste of authority and liked it, and he'd find a way to make his fortune in it. How would he feel if he knew most of the profit in Sunset came in intangibles?

"I'll tell you what, kid. When this business is done, you tell me what really led to your 'other than honorable' discharge and I'll start cutting you in on the back end. What do you say?"

"I say let's bag us a wolf . . . man. Whatever."

Hess grinned and clapped the deputy on the shoulder, hard.

TWENTY-SIX

FOR THE THIRD TIME IN TWENTY MINUTES, Nina tried Cole's cell and, again, it went straight to voicemail. This time she let it play through to the beep. She took a breath to speak, but stopped herself. Who else might be listening? Could Agent Wallace have a tap on his phone? Or could she have confiscated it? She forced herself to be calm.

"Hi Cole, it's Mom. Just calling to see what's happening, we're worried about you. Call me as soon as you can. Love you."

She hung up, wondering if it sounded as shaky as it felt. Did it sound suspicious? No, probably not. But Cole would get the point.

She heard the back door open, and a second later Ronnie walked into the kitchen. He glanced at her out of the corner of his eye but went straight to the cupboard and grabbed the aspirin.

"Well, well, well, look who showed up for work," she said.

"Not now, Ma." He popped a handful of tablets in his mouth, then cupped his hand under the faucet to swallow them.

"Everything okay?"

He ignored her while he pulled the leftover ham out of the fridge and started to put a sandwich together.

"Well?"

"Heard from Cole yet?" he asked.

"No. I just now left a message."

"Hmph. Figures."

"Ronnie, please, what's the problem?"

"You just tell me when he calls."

"Ronnie, I—"

"Is this really the time for this, Ma?" he snapped. "Because we've got a whole lot of other shit to do while he's out sorting his daddy issues."

Nina took a deep breath. Her lips shuddered as she let it out, and her eyes misted up. She wiped them away with her thumb.

"No, I suppose it's not." She looked down at his bare feet, at his grease-stained coveralls and the tangled, wet hair hanging loose around his shoulders. "You going to work like that?"

"I'm about to go change."

He finished making his sandwich in silence, then threw the extras back in the fridge and shoved the door shut. The bottles on the inside shelves rattled and he carried his sandwich toward the door.

"Soon, Ronnie. We'll talk about this soon. Okay?"

He kept his back to her. "You just tell me when Cole calls."

"Fine."

He left the kitchen.

"If you see Sean, tell him to go ahead to the gym!" she called after him.

The back door slammed.

Damn it. When this all blew over, they'd all have to take some time to talk. Decompress. Reconnect. Whatever. If Diana were here—

Shit, Diana. She didn't even know what was happening yet. Nina checked the clock. If she remembered right, Di would just be on her way to her first class. She dialed Di's cell. Three rings. Four. Come on, don't let it go to voicemail.

"Hello."

"Hi, Sweetie. Can you talk?"

A sigh. "I'm . . . studying for a test, Mom."

(I don't want to talk, Mom.)

"Is everything okay?" Nina asked.

"It will be if I can pass this test. What do you need?"

(I really don't want to talk, Mom.)

Nina leaned back on the counter, closed her eyes.

"Mom? Helloooo . . ."

"Cole's in Nevada again."

"Great. Now what?"

Again, how much to say over the phone? "The FBI agent who was here last winter is in Sunset. Cole went out to meet with her, find out what's going on."

"Okay, and?"

"And we haven't heard from him in a while."

Another sigh from Diana. "I'm sure he's fine. If he got arrested, they'd at least let him make some phone calls."

"No, it's not that. I mean, with the sheriff and all that happened with Will . . ."

"Cole's a big boy, Mom. I'm sure he can handle himself."

"I know, I just—"

"Look, this is exactly the kind of thing I went to school to get away from, remember?"

"Aren't you worried about your brother?" She put a little more edge on the words than she intended.

"Of course, but like I said, he's a big boy. If we find out there's something more, then call me."

"This isn't just some hunch, Di!"

"The professor just came in. I've got to go. Bye, Mom."

"No, Diana, wait!"

Click.

"Damn it!" Nina hung up, then redialed. Two rings, then voice mail. Nina hurled the phone into the sink. It shattered a small glass, and the phone's battery cover bounced out of the sink and skittered across the counter. She leaned against the counter and clenched her teeth as she struggled to hold back the tears.

Where had it all gone wrong? John's death? Will's? She expected the boys' behavior, but why Diana's sudden distance? She didn't even come home over her winter break; she chose, instead, to spend it at a friend's place in Texas. Nina understood the desire to spend some time in warmer weather, but did she have to spend all three weeks down there?

She pushed off the counter and walked to a back window, where she looked out toward John's hollow.

"This whole family is falling apart."

TWENTY-SEVEN

SEAN LOOKED ACROSS THE STREET at the Hammer & Lathe as he got out of his truck, and the scraps of yellow police tape affixed to the streetlamp post caught his eye. Then he noticed more cars than usual filled the parking lot, and the Dumpster around back overflowed with scrap wood and swollen garbage bags. He looked over the scene for a moment, then went into the gym.

"Hey, Sean!" Dustin greeted him. "Check it out, we're one step closer to a real cage!"

Dustin, his father Paul, and Max stood on the gym's makeshift mat and cage section and worked together to affix another segment of fencing to the side. Sean unzipped his jacket and walked over to get a better look at their handiwork.

"That's cool," he said. "I can't wait to try it out!"

"How'd you get out of the lodge?" Max asked him. "I didn't expect to see you here this time of day."

"Funny, I could say the same about you." Sean had been hoping to catch Dustin working alone so they could have a private conversation. Max would get the story eventually, of course, but he felt like it would be hard enough just one-on-one.

"Ah, I made the mistake of mentioning I had a day off to this guy, and he thought that meant he could put me to work."

"Whatever, dude. You can admit you've got nothing better to do than hang around here." Dustin punched Max on the arm, and a second later they traded blocks and phantom punches.

"Enough, guys!" Paul shouted. "If you stop acting like school children, we may still get this done this week!"

"He started it!" Max said, and Paul shot him a hard glare.

"What brings you by, Sean?" Dustin asked.

"I was hoping we could talk."

"Uh, yeah, sure. Something up?"

"Kinda. My brother and I were talking last night, and, well, I had a few questions for you."

"Go ahead," Paul said. "We got this."

Dustin stood and wiped his hands on his pants. "Why don't we go into the office?"

Sean nodded and followed him toward the back room. He felt like he got called into the principal's office.

"What's happening next door?" Sean asked as they walked. "I saw the police tape and all."

"The bikers who run the place finally crossed the line. There was some kind of fight over there last night, and the police raided the place. On the bright side, we won't have to put up with them much longer. Dad's going to evict them."

"Gee, that's too bad," he said with a laugh.

Dustin closed the office door behind Sean, motioned for him to have a seat, then walked around the desk.

"What's on your mind?"

"I had a few more questions about fighting."

"As in, you're thinking about jumping into the ring?"

"Yeah, maybe."

Dustin breathed a huge sigh of relief and sagged back in his chair. "Thank God! I was terrified you were going to tell me you didn't have the time or the money to keep working out and needed to quit."

"No, I wouldn't do that to you. The training is all I have outside the lodge right now! I just have a few concerns with the medical side."

"Ah. Well, it's not like we have an abundance of doctors here. We can get referrals to specialists in Minneapolis if there's ever a problem, but at the amateur level, we're usually on our own when it comes to health care. The big guys in the pro circuits are the ones who usually get the best treatment."

"No, it's not that. I just wonder how much of it is mandatory. For example, do I have to have an MRI?"

Dustin frowned. "Not unless you have a severe injury, I suppose. Why? Do you have some kind of medical objection?"

"Yeah, something like that."

"You're going to have to be more specific. Is it . . . religious?"

Not exactly, Sean wanted to say, but it was the easiest explanation, so he rolled with it.

"My family is into holistic medicine. I've got no problem with splints and stitches, but we try our best to avoid things like body scans, radiation and exploratory surgeries."

"Uh-huh." Dustin leaned onto his desk and considered that for a moment. "I'll tell you what. I can make a few calls, get some definitive answers for you about medical exceptions. Understand, though, there's a very real chance you can get hurt. If you get knocked out in the ring, a doctor may demand a CAT scan. If some idiot tears your shoulder out in a submission attempt, then yes, you may have to have an MRI to diagnose it. The fight commissions may even ask to see your charts before clearing you to fight. Even if you go undefeated, you're still looking at the possibility of serious injury. If that's what you're afraid of, then I have to advise you—as your friend and your coach—not to take a real fight."

Sean nodded. Not exactly what he wanted to hear, and having it broken down like that, he felt like an idiot for bringing it up. Maybe he shouldn't have let Ronnie get to him. Maybe he should just shut up and drop it.

"Yeah, you're probably right," Sean said at last.

"Can I give you one more piece of advice, if this is still about the family?"

"Of course, man."

"You need to think about whether you want to please them or please yourself. There are no half-measures, especially in a sport like this. You either need to fight and accept the consequences on both sides, or not fight and live with that decision. I'm happy to talk you through it all, but I think you've already got all the answers. You just need to follow what's in here." Dustin rapped his knuckles against this sternum.

"Yeah, you're probably right." If only Dustin knew what else was inside Sean.

Shouts erupted in the gym. Dustin stood to get a better look through the office window, and Sean twisted in his chair. Several men moved around Paul and Max. At least one of them had a gun. Dustin reached across his desk for his phone. He snatched up the handset and held it to his ear.

The door exploded open and a huge bald man came in. He pointed a dinged-up .45 at Dustin.

"Drop that fucking phone!"

Dustin dropped the phone on the desk and put his hands up.

"Both of you, out here, now!" The man gestured with the pistol and stepped out of the doorway.

Sean and Dustin followed, each holding up their hands chest high. Out in the gym, half a dozen more men in denim and leather surrounded Paul and Max. Sean recognized a few of the Lucifer's Swords members from the Hammer & Lathe. They must have called the others in for backup. Most wore the club's colors. They all carried handguns, and two of them set two large duffel bags down on the floor.

"What is this?" Paul demanded. "What do you want here?"

"Shut the fuck up," Evan said. "You said your piece, now it's our turn."

"You're doing this to change my mind? To call off the eviction? Are you out of your minds?"

"Nah, we know it's too late for that. We've got other plans." As if on cue, Slick came in from the back hallway, a smile on his face and a knife in his hand.

At that moment, Sean knew they were fucked.

Any time things got rowdy next door, every time the Swords harassed the guys at the gym, Slick could be found in the middle of it. He had a viciousness to him he didn't bother to hide, and no matter Evan's plans, Slick would take things to the next level.

"Rest of the place is clear," Slick said. "We're all good."

"Good. Lock up these other two while we have a chat with the landlord and junior here."

Three Swords, one carrying a duffle, hustled Sean and Max into the back hallway and into Dustin's tiny bedroom. Sean heard shouting out in the gym, then a gunshot and a chorus of laughter.

Sean tensed up, started to turn back, and caught a sharp blow across the back of his head. The impact sent him stumbling forward and he sprawled across Dustin's desk, sending pens and paper flying. The lamp fell off the side and crashed to the floor.

"Don't even think about it," the biker said. A big guy, bald and goateed.

Blood and adrenaline surged through Sean's muscles. He pushed himself to his feet, the urge to push out his claws and tear the man apart strong. The three guns pointed at his gut forced him to suppress it.

For now.

Baldy unzipped the duffel and rummaged inside.

The gym had fallen quiet. With luck someone outside heard the shot, but classes didn't start for hours, and the only other building within earshot was the Hammer & Lathe. Unless someone happened to be driving by, they'd be alone with the bikers.

Baldy held up a length of rope and a tattered roll of duct tape.

"Tie 'em up."

TWENTY-EIGHT

"JUST TELL ME ONE THING," Angie said. They stood in an old insurance office just down the street from the main drag. They could see her dead rental and all the other cars lined up down Main Street from here, and Cole knew the sheriff and his men had to be watching from close by.

"What's that?"

"Do you have to be naked?"

Cole laughed. "Sorry. My clothes are probably up in smoke by now."

"When you . . . change, are you still you?"

Cole looked her in the eye, read the concern there.

"Yeah, I'm still me. There's not a lot of rational thought there, it's mostly instinct. Action. But if I wouldn't hurt you now, I wouldn't hurt you after."

"So you intentionally killed all those men out in the woods?"

"I'm not a cold-blooded killer, if that's what you're getting at."

"But the potential's there."

"I thought you might want to survive all this before you finished working my case, Agent Wallace."

"I need to know what I'm working with."

She crouched on one knee at the corner of the window to watch the street. She hadn't put that shotgun down once since they started moving, and she never offered to give him one of her other guns.

Cole had already laid it all out. What more harm could be done being honest with her? If she decided to shoot him in the back, it may as well be an informed decision.

"That night at the lodge, we didn't see any other way out."

"Was that your grandfather's excuse, too?"

"What?" Cole's stomach dropped.

"Your grandfather, Gabriel Roundtree. Now he's got quite the violent past. Bank robbery, terrorism, possible murders. He's got a thick file at the Bureau."

"How do you know about my grandfather?"

"When your father bought the lodge property, he used the name Tyler, but he included a DD-214 under his birth name, John Roundtree, to take advantage of some VA opportunities. The bank still had a copy in their archives. From there it wasn't hard to find his service record, and ultimately your grandfather."

"I see." What else did she know? It sounded like they'd both have a lot of questions when they got out of Nevada.

"Where's your grandfather now?"

"Dead. He died before I was born, before my father bought the lodge. Can we handle the task at hand before you interrogate me?"

"The questions calm my nerves."

"And the answers?"

"We'll see." She set her shotgun down and stripped off her jacket.

Cole breathed in her scent, a heady mix of stale sweat, tangy chemical hygiene products, and the raw adrenaline fueling her anger and fear.

"Are you okay?" Cole asked.

"I'm burning up. I think I've about sweated myself out."

"These fires might bring help. We can escape in the confusion."

She shook her head. "No way. We need to get a move on quick or I may be dealing with heat stroke."

"If we go out there, we're walking into a trap."

"Of course we are." She pointed up to one of the roofs. "See that little bump there? That's one of our shooters. I've seen a couple more walking around on the rooftops on either side of the cars. Problem is we're running out of options fast."

"How about we beat them at their own game? I can get a burning timber from one of the houses and chuck it through one of those windows."

"You'd also make yourself a nice target. Keep thinking."

Cole examined the buildings. Some of the storefronts were contained within their own structure, most of them aging red brick and mortar. Most butted right up against one another, leaving just a few short gaps one could easily step or jump across. Facades near the top on the front side made the buildings look taller, but for the most part the stretches of roof were approximately level down the block.

"I bet I could scale one of those buildings," Cole said. "If we go up through the inside, we're sitting ducks coming through a roof door or hatch. But if I can get up from the outside, they may not expect it."

Wallace sucked air through her front teeth, then bobbed her head for a moment. "If I draw their fire, they may all come to one side, giving you a better chance."

"Then when they're busy shooting at me from the other roof, you come up through the second building."

"You really think you can hold them off that long?"

Cole shrugged. "Only one way to find out."

"Shit." Angie stretched, then leaned down and picked up the shotgun. "How long do you need to get into position?"

"Five minutes or so."

"Five it is. Just do me one favor."

"What's that?"

"Make sure you're well out of my sight before you . . . change, or transform, or whatever the hell it is you do. I'd hate to panic and blow you away when I need you."

TWENTY-NINE

THE BIKERS TOOK SEAN'S CELL PHONE and tied him to Dustin's chair, his arms bound to the armrests and his ankles bound to the center column. They taped his mouth and rolled him back into the corner as they bound Max and lashed him to Dustin's cot. He strained against the ropes to test them; maybe he'd be able to use his claws to cut loose, but no way he'd just break free.

"That oughta do it," Baldy said. "Now dose 'em up."

The skinny younger kid reached into the duffel and pulled out a vial of milky fluid, then took two syringes out of a bundle in his pocket.

Sean's heart quickened while Skinny drew fluid into the first syringe. He struggled and thrashed, but the ropes held tight. He should have risked a transformation. At least it might have given him a fighting chance.

"Sorry, bro," Skinny said. "But don't worry, in a minute you'll feel alright."

Skinny shoved Sean up against the wall and pinned his arm with one knee. Sean couldn't see past Skinny's arm, but he felt the needle punch through the skin on his forearm. The site burned, then heat raced up his arm and radiated through his chest. His heart hammered faster and faster, and a wave of ecstasy washed over him.

Sean closed his eyes. His head lolled forward. Max's muffled protests and the metallic rattle of the cot sounded muffled and distorted, as if someone had dropped him into a pool. But the gym didn't have a pool.

Did it?

Sean opened his eyes and his vision swam with color. A huge face filled his view, blowing up like an overinflated balloon. The head spoke, its voice carrying no words, just a long caress in his ears. Then the head zoomed out, fading out and out almost to a pinprick. A hollow boom rang through the room and the world went dark but for a slash of light across the floor.

• • •

"Don't worry, this won't take much longer." Evan punched Paul in the face this time. The landlord's head bounced off the segment of cage they had tied him to and lolled forward. He mumbled something toward his chest as blood dripped to the mat below.

"Stop!" Dustin pleaded. The Smith machine the Swords tied him to skidded an inch across the concrete floor as he tried to reach his father, despite the bleeding bullet wound in his right thigh. "You're killing him!"

"Soon enough, kid." Evan turned and shouted over his shoulder. "How's it coming?"

"Almost done," Leland replied from the office. He had stashed some raw meth in the back of a file cabinet, and now spread some of their special mix and a few needles around the desktop. In a moment he'd trash the office, make it look like it had been ransacked.

Paul mumbled something again. Evan grabbed his hair and yanked his head back.

"What was that?"

"Why—" something-something, mumble-mumble.

"I think I punched him retarded, boys."

The Swords laughed.

"He said, 'why are you doing this?' " Dustin said.

Evan craned his neck to look Paul in the eye. "That right?"

A nod.

Evan punched him again. Paul's head snapped around to his right and he let out a sob.

"It's simple, really," Evan said, turning to address Dustin. "I have a business to protect, and you tried to fuck it all up. Now we've got to cover our tracks, and put John Law onto another path. The easiest way to do that is to make it look like you've been the drug dealers all along. Only problem is, we can't be playing the I-said-you-said game, so you and Pops here need to be out of the picture."

He backhanded Paul for emphasis. The wet smack echoed through the gym.

"So you torture us first?"

Evan shrugged. "I never said it wasn't personal. Besides, junkies do some heinous shit when they need their fix. This helps sell the story."

"It'll never work. They've got my 911 call from last night. If I were dealing, why would I call the cops so close to my own place?"

"Who cares? Let the cops take down the perceived competition, maybe? They found nothing; they got nothing. We're just a motorcycle club full of guys looking to go legit building furniture, and the stereotype continues to get perpetrated upon us."

Evan put another solid punch into Paul's gut. Paul gagged.

"Whoop, look out! He's gonna blow!"

Evan danced back several steps just as Paul threw up all over the mat.

"Is that biscuits and gravy? Don't you know that shit's bad for you at your age?"

Another round of laughter from the Swords. Evan lifted Paul's head again, turned it back and forth to examine him. Then he let Paul's head drop.

"He's done. You're up, Slick."

"Right on." Slick stuck his pistol into his waistband and flicked his knife open. "How you want it done?"

"Messy. Junkies, remember?"

"No prob."

Dustin screamed and pleaded and thrashed in his bonds as Slick strode across the mat. Slick took extra care to straddle the blood and vomit at his feet, then braced Paul against the cage with his left hand. He cocked his knife at his hip, then looked over his shoulder and winked at Dustin.

Shunk-shunk-shunk.

Two deep holes in Paul's gut and one under the ribs. One more long scream from Dustin as Slick stepped away. Paul, already well out of it, died with a shallow gasp.

"You mother fuckers!" Dustin screamed. The Smith machine rattled and clanked with his rage. "Untie me and let's finish this like men!"

"Oh, I'm sure you'd like that, wouldn't you?" Evan asked. "Sadly, my guys can't have a mark on 'em if their story's gonna hold. Your story, meanwhile, is going to play out a bit differently. See, I'm thinking they had to cut on you a while to get you to give up your stash."

"Mother fuckers." Dustin sagged against the machine. "You dirty mother fuckers . . ."

Slick approached him, grinning and brandishing his bloodied knife, but Dustin could only stare at his father's lifeless body dangling from the cage.

THIRTY

NINA TAPPED Agent Wallace's business card against the desk blotter. She had called the mobile number twice in the past hour. Both times, it went straight to voice mail. She kept her message simple the first time: "This is Nina Tyler. Please call me back as soon as possible." She left her direct phone number at the lodge. The second time, she just hung up.

She looked at the office number again, then reached for the phone. Dialed. A man answered on the second ring.

"Special Agent Humphrey, can I help you?"

"Yes, hi, I was trying to reach Agent Angela Wallace?"

"I'm sorry, she's on leave right now. Is there something I can help you with?"

Nina blinked. "On leave? I don't understand. Why is she . . . ?"

Shit, don't say too much, she thought.

"I'm sorry, ma'am, all I can tell you is she's not on duty. I'm handling her cases."

If she's not on duty, then why is she in Nevada? What's she doing with Hess? And Cole? What in the hell is she up to?

"Who's calling, please?" Humphrey asked.

"Oh, just a friend of hers, that's all. I'll try her another time." Nina hung up, probably a little too hard.

Shit. She dropped her head into her hands. This didn't make sense. Either she was up to something, or Wallace and Cole were both in trouble.

The phone rang. Her heart jumped as she looked up and saw the flashing LED next to the same line she'd used to call the FBI. She wondered if it could be Wallace, but didn't dare answer in case it were Humphrey ringing her back.

She hit the button for another line, picked up, called Ronnie's cell.

"Yeah, Ma." He already sounded exasperated.

"Get your brother and meet me back at the office."

"Sean's not back yet."

"What? He was supposed to be back a while ago!"

"I don't know what to tell you, Ma. He was supposed to help me with the electrical on Lot 5, but I haven't seen him."

She closed her eyes, clenched her fist. Damn it, this is not the time!

"Forget it," she said. "Come back to the office. We'll stop and pick him up on the way."

"On the way where? What's going on, Ma?"

"We're going to Nevada. Now."

A second of silence, then, "About goddamn time. I'll be right there."

"And find Amy. We'll need her to cover the office."

"Will do."

Nina hung up, grabbed a light jacket, and went outside to wait. She paced the gravel drive out front, back and forth, back and forth. With luck they could still catch a flight and hit Nevada by late evening. Worst case, maybe they could charter a flight, get there sooner. Maybe even find a small airport closer to Sunset.

Then what? Storm the sheriff's office? Scour the town? Or lay low and look for anything out of the ordinary first?

Screw it, they could talk about it on the flight. Now what in the hell was taking Ronnie so long?

Five very long minutes later, Ronnie pulled up in one of the lodge pickups. Amy climbed out of the passenger seat.

"We shouldn't be long," Nina said, "Don't worry about overtime or any of that, we will, of course, make sure you're taken care of."

"Hey, don't worry about it, Mrs. Tyler. I'm happy to help out."

Nina stepped past Amy and grabbed the inside of the doorframe, then caught a whiff of something. She froze, looked over at Amy.

"Is something wrong, Mrs. Tyler?"

Ronnie made an effort to look straight out through the windshield, but she could see him trying to watch her out of the corner of his eye.

"Never mind," Nina said. "I'm sure it's nothing. Thanks again."

Nina climbed into the cab and slammed the door shut. She watched Amy in the passenger side mirror as Ronnie pulled away from the office and drove toward the lodge gate. Amy watched them leave, then went into the office.

Ronnie had a long string of broken hearts and burned bridges stretching all the way back to high school. Now she smelled him all over Amy. It didn't seem quite right for his scent to have rubbed off on her in the short drive to the office, and now she realized they both smelled like the freebie soaps and shampoos they put in the lodge cabins.

How long had this been going on? She hoped like hell they were at least being discrete in front of the visitors. Did Cole know about this? Did Sean?

She seethed in the passenger seat. The family should be talking about these things. They'd all grown too distant from one another. When this all blew over, they would all have to sit down and hash things out. Or even better, take some time to get away together. Regroup and recharge. She'd even drag Diana off that college campus for a few days, whether they could time it with spring break or not. Once Cole comes home, things will change.

First things first. If that sheriff had taken another of her boys from her, she'd damn well kill him herself this time.

THIRTY-ONE

THE SUN BEAT DOWN HOT ON ANGIE'S BACK, obliterating any shadow she might have used for cover as she crept down the back alley behind the Main Street businesses. The massive smoke column rising from the other side of town cast its shadow in the wrong direction, and the wispy tendrils of smoke snaking their way down the street did little to cover her movements. If one of Hess's men leaned over that rooftop with a good rifle and a steady hand, it would be all over.

She picked up the pace behind the last building, shifting from stealth to speed. Her eyes flitted from the back door of the last shop to the roof across the street and back again. Just thirty more seconds, she told herself. Her dead car leaned on the curb just around the corner, and the shooters would be keeping an eye out for her.

She crouched near the concrete stoop at the back door and aimed the shotgun skyward. Still no movement on the rooftops. She kept the shotgun aimed high as she reached for the door handle, then twisted.

Locked. She braced herself and put more muscle into it. Still nothing. She pulled. The wooden frame creaked and groaned.

Enough. She didn't have time for this shit. She needed cover, and the shooting would start soon enough anyway.

She pulled the .44 out of her pocket, pointed it just behind the strike plate, turned her head, and squeezed the trigger. The blast echoed down the alley and the door latch exploded out of the frame. Someone shouted from up high as she pocketed the .44 and pulled the door handle. It snagged for a split second—just long enough to drive a spike of panic into her chest—then opened with the crunch and crackle of splintering wood. She rammed a shoulder through the door and rushed inside.

The darkness and dust of the interior hallway swallowed her up. She spun and backed up to the far wall, pointed the shotgun back down the corridor. Her breathing sounded loud and harsh in her head. More vague shouts from outside, but nobody appeared in the doorway.

The dim hall led away to her right and out to the front room. She let the shotgun lead the way, duckwalking with purpose. Diffuse light from the papered-over front windows revealed an abandoned storefront full of magazine and greeting card racks. Her footsteps kicked up great motes of dust. She paused for a beat to watch for shadows on the front window, then moved down the aisle to the front door. She reached out with her left hand and twisted the lock. The dry mechanism rasped as it turned, but finally clicked open. She grabbed the door handle, then froze and looked up. No bell.

She pulled the door open a few inches and peered outside. The street was quiet. Still. She hooked the door with her foot and shouldered the shotgun as she stepped across the threshold. Outside, she eased the door shut with her trailing foot and pressed herself to the window on the left side.

Twin columns of brick flanked the entranceway. She held the shotgun vertically across her chest and faced the column, then leaned over for a quick peek around the corner, just long enough to take in the long line of cars parked nose-to-tail down the street. No sign of the bad guys.

If it were her, she'd be on the roof or waiting in the shops along the street. She leaned out again, looked up, and saw someone leaning over the roof ledge with a rifle. She darted back into the entranceway. Now she just had to flush them out for Cole.

Piece of cake.

Angie chuckled. She could just imagine the new scenarios she could write for the Academy combat trainers after this one.

No time to reconsider. She leaned the shotgun around the corner, shouldered it, sighted down the barrel with her good eye. The rifleman's head turned as she fired, pumped, fired again. He went flat and she ducked back around the corner. Lots of shouting.

Gunshots. The plate glass broke and huge shards crashed to the sidewalk.

Cole had better get his ass in gear.

• • •

Cole repeated the plan to himself:

Wait for the shots, find Hess and his men. Wait for the shots, find Hess and his men. Wait for the shots. Find Hess. Wait. Find Hess.

His flesh and bones shifted and twisted. Fur emerged across his skin.

Wait for the shots.

He dropped to the floor as his legs reconfigured themselves. His spine stretched and popped as his tail moved into place. A familiar pain wracked his body.

Find Hess.

He welcomed the pain this time, relished the tension in his claws.

Wait for the shots.

Find Hess.

He could already smell the foul cigar smoke, already taste the blood.

Find the men.

The beast stood and stretched the kinks out of its muscles. It dared not howl. It knew this was a time for hunting, a time for stealth.

Find the men.

Yes, find the men. Before the fire came, before they killed the woman. She would find them first, bring their guns to her. Then he would find them.

Wait for the shots.

Kill them all.

THIRTY-TWO

FIRE BURNED THROUGH SEAN'S VEINS. He breathed in heaving gasps, like an old train building steam. He tried to stand, but something held him back.

Rope?

It bound his arms and legs to something. A chair? Everything felt fuzzy, distant. The desk behind him, the bed next to him. Not his, but familiar somehow.

Something squirmed on a bed next to him, whimpered. The dark room reeked of sweat. He could hear men talking, their voices muted and distorted. Muddy. The strip of light on the floor burned laser bright, then swam and receded to the barest pinprick before zooming back in again.

Someone screamed. Lots of shouting. Anger. Rage.

A new scent. Blood?

Yes, blood. Whatever this place was, he had to get out. He strained and pulled against the ropes. The chair squeaked and groaned but held him tight. He tried to call out but something covered his mouth, a strip of cloth. He chewed at it. His muscles stretched and his bones twisted. His saliva soaked the rag and he chewed and chewed. His claws pushed through his fingertips and he raked at the ropes around his wrists. His teeth grew long and sharp, and in seconds the rag turned to tatters in his mouth. He let them fall as he pulled and strained against the ropes.

The thing on the bed screamed, the sound muffled. The bed clattered and clacked against the floor and the wall.

Voices outside the door got louder. One of them laughed.

The noise brought them. Sean willed the thing on the bed to be silent. Still it screamed.

He shook the rag loose from his mouth. He growled a threat at the struggling thing. It thrashed and screamed. Sean raked his bonds.

In seconds he would be free, and he would silence that thing forever.

◆ ◆ ◆

Slick smeared his bloody blade across Dustin's face. Reddened tears streamed down his cheeks, as he looked up at Slick with rage.

"Your macho bullshit's all gone now, isn't it?" Slick asked.

Dustin's upper lip trembled. He strained against the ropes, against the Smith machine's rigid frame, but they held.

Slick laughed. "Oh, he's mad now."

"Let's get it over with," Evan said.

"I thought you said we had to cut on him a while?"

"Yeah, but we don't have all day. Just make it look good."

Slick heaved a deep sigh. He crossed his arms and sized up Dustin like a sculptor examining a slab of marble. He turned and stepped to one side for a new perspective.

"Goddamn it, Slick!"

"Okay! Shit!" He leaned in close to Dustin and winked. "Spoilsport."

Then he started to carve.

His blade flashed in the fluorescent light as it sliced and stabbed and slashed. Dustin grunted against the pain at first, but in seconds the cumulative pain kicked in and he cried out again and again as his own blood coursed down his body and pooled at his feet. Slick ignored the blood flecking his hands and arms and spraying his face and chest. He went at Dustin faster and harder, cutting deeper with each pass.

At last Slick got tired of Dustin's screaming. He pressed a palm into the fighter's forehead, shoved his head back, and plunged his knife deep into Dustin's throat. Dustin's cries died and his eyes went wide. Blood poured out of his mouth and he made choking and gagging sounds for several seconds as his head drooped, then lolled free on his shoulders. His body went slack against the ropes.

Slick took his knife back and wiped the blade on his jeans.

"Jesus, Slick," Evan said. The other Swords tried to stand their ground, but they averted their eyes from the bloody mess.

"What?" Slick asked. "You said cut on him a while!"

"Yeah, but . . ." Evan shook his head. "Let's just get to work and get the fuck out of here."

◆ ◆ ◆

Bobby swallowed hard against the vomit in his throat. He didn't dare puke and turn Slick—or even Uncle Evan, for that matter—on him.

He was no idiot. He knew the MC got into some heavy shit. Slinging dope and making money and banging broads didn't always come easy, and he expected the occasional flirtation with violence and John Law coming down on them.

But this? This sick shit didn't make any sense.

He wanted to run, to get the hell out and jump on a bike and ride out of town. Fuck the patch, fuck the MC, fuck Uncle Evan. Go back to Chicago, or maybe down to Nashville and lay low until he could start fresh.

But that would be weakness. If he turned and ran from the gym, they'd beat the shit out of him. If he fled to Chicago, they'd find him and kill him. Live a Sword, die a Sword, as Uncle Evan had warned him.

If only he could have seen this coming, seen how bad it could really get.

"Bobby, you okay?"

His head snapped up. He looked directly at Uncle Evan, and tried hard to ignore what remained of the fight club guy in his peripheral vision.

"I'm fine."

"You look a little green, kid."

Slick laughed. "Guess we popped his cherry good!"

"I'm fine," he insisted.

Evan regarded him for a moment. Bobby wiped an arm across his forehead to get the sweat off.

"Get the drugs," Evan said.

The Swords picked up their satchels and removed the packets of crystalline flakes. At Evan's instruction, they ransacked the office, dumping the file cabinets and ripping out the desk drawers. They spilled some flakes on the floor and left a broken packet beneath one of the cabinets.

In the gym, Slick slashed two of the punching bags and let their contents leak out all over the floor. He took the cap off the base of another punching bag shaped like a buff fighter with no arms, then wrestled it to the ground. Water glugged out and spread across the floor.

Bobby wiped his hands on his pants and retreated to a corner. Two bodies and a huge mess. Unreal.

"What about the guys in back?" Sid asked.

Bobby winced. He'd almost forgotten about them.

"We're almost done here. Prep a few needles and we'll bring 'em out."

Meth ODs. Fuck. He'd almost rather have the knife.

Well, not if Slick held it. But still.

These poor bastards are in for a world of hurt.

THIRTY-THREE

"SOMETHING'S WRONG," Denton said. He raised his head from his scope and surveyed the street below, then got up and walked to the other side of the roof to look down.

McCabe held a bead on the street, and on the rooftop across from them, Sam returned fire while Lewis ducked low and tried to act as a spotter.

"What're you talking about?" Hess crouched near McCabe and watched as Denton braced a foot on the ledge and leaned over the side to look down the alley.

"She's a fed, right? She knows that shotgun isn't going to hit anything at this distance. She's drawing our fire."

"A distraction. Shit!" Hess stood and pulled his pistol. He backed away from McCabe and took tentative looks over the edge at the cars below. Then he cupped his hands to his mouth. "Lewis!"

Lewis's head snapped around.

"Watch your back!" he shouted as Sam snapped off another round.

Lewis put a hand to his ear.

"I said watch your back! Tyler's on the move!"

Lewis nodded and ran to check the hatch near an old air conditioner unit near the center of the roof.

Hess risked a further lean over the roof, eyeballed the front doors of the shops below. A tattered awning over one door concealed the entry, but otherwise he didn't see anything.

A shotgun blast roared down the street. Buckshot peppered the brick wall a few feet below Sam and to his right. Sam returned another shot, then rolled away from the ledge to swap in a fresh magazine.

"Do you see Tyler?" Hess shouted.

"Just the woman." Sam worked a round into the chamber and returned to his firing position.

Hess continued around the perimeter and looked around the far side of the building. Denton met him at the far corner.

"Anything?" Hess asked.

"Nope. Any chance he bailed on her?"

"After coming this far for her? I doubt it."

"Then maybe she took him out?"

Hess snorted out a laugh. "We should be so lucky. Keep your eyes open. That sumbitch is out there somewhere."

• • •

The beast stopped to listen to the gunfire. Some of the shots came from the street, but most echoed across the rooftops. He sniffed at the air, then loped down the alley and crouched beneath a service ladder before leaping and snagging the bottom rung with both hands. He pulled himself up and scrambled toward the roof.

The gunshots grew louder. Men shouted to one another.

He would silence them all, and the woman would be safe.

The beast leapt over the edge of the roof and saw the two men on the other side, one lying prone with a rifle and the other walking across the rooftop toward him. The beast sprinted toward them, his feet thudding across the rubbery surface.

The walking man looked over his shoulder, then his eyes went wide and he stumbled in his haste to escape. The beast plowed through him, never slowing as he seized the man by the throat and thigh and hoisted him up high overhead. The beast's claws dug deep into his flesh to find purchase and the man dropped his gun.

Three more long strides and the beast hurled the man off the roof. He spun headlong over the side and plummeted to the street below where his scream was cut off with a sickening thud and the crash of shattered glass.

The rifleman saw his partner fall, then rolled over in time to see the beast fall upon him. He cried out as the beast's claws raked across his arms, flaying the muscles and destroying his grip.

Shouts broke out across the street. Another man pointed a rifle at the beast. His first panicked shot went wide.

The beast grabbed the fallen rifle and hurled it toward the other rooftop. The other man ducked as the rifle struck the ledge. The stock cracked and it spun over the side and tumbled down to the street.

More shots. The beast lifted the rifleman and held him in front of his chest like a shield as he ran for the huge metal air conditioning unit. The other men kept shooting. A bullet cracked past the beast's ear, and another punched into the rifleman's back. The man gasped and squirmed.

The beast reached cover and slammed the rifleman against the wall. The man's eyes closed and his breath came in hitching breaths. The beast finished him with a claw swipe across the throat and threw the body back into the open.

Bullets punched the metal walls of the AC unit and struck something solid inside. The beast crouched low and moved across the back side. He knew Hess was over there. He wanted to leap across the roofs and tear the man limb from limb, but he knew it would leave him wide open to Hess's bullets.

No, this still called for stealth and cunning. The beast ran for the ladder and leapt over the side of the roof. Bullets tore through the air above him as he half slid, half jumped down the ladder and to the alley.

◆ ◆ ◆

Angie shoved back through the door and around to her right, then hopped up onto the display platform behind the front window and backed against the wall. She flipped the shotgun over and pushed the last six shells into the magazine, then pumped one into the chamber.

She listened for a moment, then dropped to one knee, swung the shotgun around through the broken window, took quick aim, and fired. The shotgun punched her shoulder and she rolled with it back into cover. A second later, a bullet struck the floor two feet in front of her.

This guy's being very patient, she thought. Of course, he only had to keep her occupied until his own guys could respond. They'd move into position, maybe come in the back door, and it would be all over. Cole or no Cole, she had to get a move on.

A sudden, peculiar scream broke out, punctuated by a loud crash. Another scream followed, then gunshots. She flinched away from the window, but no bullets came her way.

The screams continued. No time to think, just go-go-go. She glanced around the corner, saw the sniper had gone, then jumped out the window and sprinted across the street toward her disabled car. A searing pain shot through her hip and she limped the last two steps across the sidewalk and slammed herself against the wall.

Angie aimed the shotgun straight upward. Nobody came to the edge looking for her. She moved to the corner, peered around at the cars and saw the cruiser with the smashed lightbar and collapsed roof, and the twisted human leg sticking out over the shattered windshield. She checked both roofs, but saw nobody despite the gunshots ringing out above her.

It only took a second to cross the storefront and slip into the entryway. Once there she eyeballed the rooftops once more, then rolled out to the next door, the entrance for the offices or apartment above the shop. A solid kick made short work of the weather-worn wooden door, and she limped up the steps as fast as she could, keeping the shotgun trained on the landing the whole way.

THIRTY-FOUR

THE THING ON THE BED squirmed and thrashed and screamed its muffled screams. It reeked of sweat and urine, the stenches of terror and weakness.

The beast's bonds broke. The chair fell back and hit the wall as the beast pounced on the bed. Its claws shredded cloth, tore flesh and snagged bone. Blood sprayed its face and chest, soaked its fur and splattered the walls. The noisy, terrified thing thrashed beneath the beast, then fell still and silent.

Pounding roared through the room.

The beast froze, snapped its head around to the light, now eclipsed in places by moving shadows. Hesitant voices, the words lost to the beast's own heart pounding in its ears.

More pounding. A heavy fist on wood.

"What the hell's going on in there?" A human voice. Male. Angry.

A metallic rattle. The click of a door latch.

The beast turned toward the light. He crouched, ready to spring. A vertical sliver of light erupted in front of him. More light washed into the room.

The beast leapt.

Bright light burned its eyes, but it could smell and feel the two men in the hallway as it collided with them. The men screamed. An explosion hammered its ears as it brought the two men to the floor and ripped into them with claws and teeth. Its eyes found focus through the fine red mist. One man lay dead at its feet, eyes wide with terror. The other clawed his way up the hall, smearing blood across the white tile and choking on his own blood.

The beast seized the crawling man, digging its claws into his shoulder and the meat of his back. The man screamed as the beast lifted him into the air, then went silent as the beast slammed him first into one wall, then the opposite.

More men appeared at the end of the hall. They skidded to a halt when they saw the beast, their eyes wide and mouths open. Most ran. One pointed a pistol at the beast. Its muzzle flashed and two shots rattled the hall.

One bullet zipped past the beast's shoulder. The other punched into the dead man it still held against the wall.

The shooter ran.

The beast dropped the body and gave chase.

• • •

Bobbly flinched so hard at the first gunshot he dropped the bag of meth. It hit the floor with a heavy slap and the white crystals burst through a crack in one side and fanned out across the office carpeting.

"Shit!" He looked out into the gym, saw the others pulling their weapons and moving toward the hallway. He looked down at the meth, wondered if he should pick it up, find a vacuum, or just leave it be.

Then he heard the screaming and the noise. He went to the office door. Jesus, a raid? Who could know they were here? Did they trip a security alarm? Leave a phone open? He watched Evan and Slick and the others converge on the hallway, their backs to the wall flanking the door.

Bobby half expected a SWAT team to charge into the gym. The doors would suddenly go up, the entrance door would explode inward, and the place would be swarming with cops. He suddenly couldn't breathe. Should he run for a door? Hit the deck? He didn't have a gun and sure as shit didn't want to shoot anyone.

Oh God, the bodies. No cop would see that shit and go easy on them.

Evan mouthed a one-two-three to Sid, then they charged into the hallway. Bobby winced when they screamed and came running back out, Evan shooting back down the hallway.

What the fuck could these guys be afraid of?

Then the nightmare barreled into the gym, all fur and blood and teeth. Bobby's brain couldn't put a name to it, he just backed against the wall and tried to be invisible as it tackled Sid in the middle of the room and tore him apart.

Gunshots echoed around the gym. The office window beside Bobby shattered and a bullet smacked into the brick above his head. He hit the deck.

Get the hell out of here you asshole!

He didn't think, just scrambled to his feet and ran. A cold spike of terror went through his gut when the beast howled and he hoped and prayed with all his might that it hadn't spotted him. His back tensed up in anticipation of the thing tearing into him, but it never came.

His shoulder struck the hallway wall with a crunch and pain lanced up his neck. More screams behind him, more gunshots, and again that ungodly fucking howl. In front of him, bodies and blood. He sprinted toward them, vaulted them like a fucking Olympian hurdler.

His heel landed in blood and slipped out from beneath him. He threw his hands out behind him as he fell back. He expected to hit floor and instead landed on something hot, wet and squishy. Something went crunch beneath his ass.

Bobby didn't dare look. He felt a surge of vomit in his throat and swallowed hard as he threw himself forward.

His sneakers slipped and slid through blood until he got them beneath him and he found grip at last. He sprinted headlong for the fire exit at the end of the hall.

The exit lever made a loud clack as he struck it. The door held for half a second, then flew open with his weight. The alarm buzzer box went off, its droning scream drowning out the chaos in the gym.

The door closed behind Bobby, muffling the buzzer as he sprinted straight down the alley, past the Dumpsters, and around the corner toward the Hammer & Lathe. He fished his keys out of his pocket when he hit the street and jumped the curb.

His bike started with a roar. He gunned the throttle, dropped into first and engaged the clutch. The front wheel kicked up and the bike lurched forward, nearly dumping him off the back side. He didn't dare release the grips and he damn near broke his ankle steadying himself as the bike roared across the parking lot. The bike already hit twenty when he leaned hard into the turn onto the street. His wheels missed the opposite curb by inches.

Then he was off through the industrial park, and he didn't dare look back.

◆ ◆ ◆

Leland almost made the door. He died with his hands on the latch bar, and now sprawled in front of the threshold, the door propped open on his wrist and his dead eye staring out into daylight.

Slick expended his ammo firing in panic. He spent his last seconds trying to find another gun, another magazine, anything to fight back with after the wolf thing cut off his escape and slaughtered Leland. He thought he spotted Sid's gun lying beside the mat at the old man's feet just as the creature pounced on him.

Slick knew he took a wrong turn running for the exit. He couldn't see past all the equipment, though he was headed the right way and instead found the big garage doors. It took him several seconds to find the sliding lock, and he yanked on it three times before realizing a padlock held it firm. No sign of a key. He went to the second door, found the same lock and an identical padlock. Also closed.

He ducked behind a rack of dumbbells near the wall. Whether he ran for the hallway or the front door, he had to get past the wolf thing. Maybe he could stay low, let it leave. Just like fights in the prison yard or on the cell block: shut the fuck up, stay out of sight, let things blow over.

His thumb pressed into the ridged curve at the base of his knife blade, the only outward nervous tick he allowed himself. His thumb braced the knife and gave him control.

The wolf thing stood. Slick ducked lower and peeked between two dumbbells to watch it shake its head and shoulders like a wet dog. A fine red spray rained down all around it.

The wolf thing sniffed the air with a wet, snuffling sound. It dropped to all fours and crawled out of Slick's sightline. He didn't dare move and catch its attention. The snuffling continued for a few seconds, then stopped. A low growl took its place. Footfalls approached Slick's position. Claws clicked on the concrete floor.

Closer. Closer still.

Slick bowed his head for just a second. He'd been cornered before. He had a knife then, too, and he'd cut his way free. He looked at the blade in his hand. No reason he couldn't do it again.

The wolf thing stalked past the first garage door.

Go time. Slick stood and held up his knife. He stepped to one side to keep the dumbbell rack between him and the wolf thing.

It stopped, rose to its hind legs. Its lips curled up and back to reveal rows of sharp, red-stained teeth. Its growl deepened.

Slick licked the sweat off his upper lip. If it growled, it had a throat. It breathed like any other animal. Put his knife in there, it would go down. Play it careful and time it right, he could make it through this.

The wolf thing tensed, then sprang toward him.

Slick brought his knife up in a high arc.

He never finished the motion. The wolf thing moved too fast and he felt its claws in his arm a split second before the jaws clamped down on the side of his neck.

His back hit the wall and the wolf thing's weight crushed the breath out of him.

Then it thrashed. His legs flew through the air like a rag doll's and struck the dumbbell rack. He lost track of everything but the blinding, searing pain shooting through his entire body. He willed his arm to fight back, to stab this thing in its furry guts.

Did it work? Didn't matter.

Too late now.

THIRTY-FIVE

"LOOKS LIKE HE'S STILL HERE." Ronnie pulled up beside Sean's old black Wrangler and parked. "Maybe he just lost track of time?"

"We're about to find out." Nina climbed out of the truck and slammed the door shut behind her. They could leave the Jeep here, take the pickup to the airport.

Ronnie grabbed her arm and held her back a step.

"What is it?"

"Shh!" He pointed to the door just ahead of them.

Nina saw now the door stood open a few inches. She looked down and saw the pale, bloodied hand wedged in the gap.

"I'm going in," Ronnie said, and ran for the door.

"No, wait!"

Nina reached for his jacket but it slipped through her fingers. He ran to the door and opened it, then jumped over the body on the other side and disappeared into the gym. She followed him and opened the door with caution, half expecting to hear fighting or conflict.

Instead she heard Ronnie calling out "Sean? Sean!?"

She looked down at the body in the door. There could be no mistaking the ragged tears inflicted by bestial claws, or the bite pattern across the back of the man's neck.

Oh, Sean, what have you done?

The rich, heady scent of blood overwhelmed the interior. She saw the old man hanging limp from the cage, his face beaten and the front of his shirt drenched with blood. She saw another man hanging from a steel frame, his face and chest cut to ribbons. More brutalized bodies on the floor, their blood splattered everywhere.

Ronnie came running out of the office and ran for the back hallway.

"Ronnie, wait!"

He stopped and looked at her.

"Don't touch anything."

A curt nod, and he was off again.

Nina stepped around the blood as best she could. The timing of this could not be any more wrong. Cole would have to fend for himself until she could resolve this.

Whatever this was.

She examined the body in the center of the room. He'd been ravaged like the man in the door, and a handgun—

its slide locked back on an empty magazine—laid on the floor several feet away. She looked around the room, then spotted the bullet holes in the office window and in the wall above it.

Could Sean have caught one of those bullets? Is that what triggered this?

The man wore a denim jacket covered with patches, and she realized it matched the one worn by the body in the door. The man's outstretched right arm had no blood on it, so she grabbed the sleeve and lifted him onto his side. On his back, flowing banners reading "Lucifer's Swords, MC" and "Chicago" surrounded a colorful image of a sword with a flaming blade. She eased the body back to the ground and brushed her fingers off on her pant leg as she stood. Another body across the room had an identical jacket.

Nina walked to within a few feet of the body hanging from the big weight rack. She could see now that his wounds were different, too clean to have come from Sean's claws. Someone had worked him over with a blade, a knife or maybe a straight razor. She couldn't read the logo on his t-shirt, but he wore a pair of trunks and had no shoes, and she guessed he must be a gym member.

Ronnie reemerged from the back hallway, his face pale. He carried a rolled-up wad of clothing in his hand.

"There are three more bodies back there," he said. "One's strapped to a cot. I think it's Sean's friend Max.

These look like Sean's clothes, and they were scattered around a chair back there."

"No sign of Sean?"

"Other than the mess? No. But there's more. There are drugs in the office. Looks like meth or heroine or something."

"Shit." If the cops weren't here yet, they would be soon. And it wouldn't take long for them to start comparing the bodies in the gym to those of the gangsters at the lodge last fall.

Ronnie came to her side. "We need to find Sean."

"I'll do it. You get his truck back to the lodge, wait and see if he shows up there."

"Fuck the truck! We need to—"

Nina slapped Ronnie hard across the face. The sound echoed like a gunshot around the gym. His eyes went wide with fury.

"This is not the time to argue with me!" she shouted. She took the clothes from him and rummaged through the jeans until she found Sean's keys. "We need to distance ourselves from this situation now. You get the truck back to the lodge and it should keep the police off our backs for a while. I will find Sean because we don't know what caused this and what kind of shape he's in."

"Ma, I can find him as easily as you can!"

"If he's lost it, who do you think he'll respond to better, you or me?"

Ronnie's nostrils flared. His fingers flexed and relaxed. She could almost smell the anger radiating from him, the desire to lash out. He held it back, though, and only nodded.

"Good. Let's go."

THIRTY-SIX

HESS HELD HIS .45 AT THE READY and scanned the roofline all around them. He just needed Tyler to show his head for a second so he could put a silver bullet through it. He remembered the day Tyler told him silver only worked in the movies, but Hess wasn't one to take chances.

Besides which they worked just fine on Tyler's brother and on Marcus Rice.

"This isn't happening, this isn't happening, holy shit this isn't happening," McCabe muttered over and over again.

"Hold it together, Tim!" Hess snapped.

"Hey, fuck you, man! You got me into this mess! I knew I shouldn't have come out here with you!"

"I said hold it together, goddamn it! Stay sharp and you'll still walk out of here with me."

McCabe shook his head, muttered under his breath.

Denton at least stayed cool. He swapped his AR-15 for the shotgun in the corner, ready for close encounters. He held it at his shoulder and always looked straight down the barrel as he stepped slow and easy around the roof. Perfect control. Hess stepped up beside him and covered his back.

"You okay, kid?" Hess asked.

"I'll shit my pants later, Sir."

Hess chuckled. "You just get that thing in your sights. Bullets'll drop it, sure enough."

"We should just give them the keys," McCabe said.

"Why's that?"

"They just want to get out of here, right? Fuck it! Throw the keys over the side and let 'em go!"

"It's not that simple. What makes you think that thing will let any of us leave alive?"

"Uh-uh, it's you they want. I'm getting out of here." McCabe went to the pile of keys and crouched down to search for his own.

"Think about this, Tim. We're in a defensible position. You're a sitting duck if you go down there."

"I just need to make it to my truck. I'll take my chances."

"Goddamn it, Tim! Stop!"

McCabe hurried for the roof hatch.

"Let him go." Denton kept his voice low.

"What?"

"Maybe he'll flush them out."

Hess watched McCabe pull the hatch open and look down the hole. He leaned over, cautious, swept the small utility room below with his rifle. Hess felt better with more eyeballs up top, but maybe Denton had a point.

"Tim!"

McCabe stopped, one foot on the top rung of the ladder.

"Be careful."

McCabe nodded. "Good luck, sheriff." Then he pulled the hatch shut over him.

• • •

Angie pressed her back to the wall on her left as she climbed the last few steps. A narrow hallway led off in both directions, and she peered around the corner to her right. She could see three doors, one of them open and letting in just enough light to see by. Offices, she thought, or maybe apartments. One had to have a way to get to the roof.

She paused on the top step to listen for a moment, then swung around and dropped to one knee on the faded, dusty hall carpeting and pointed the shotgun down the hall to the left. Two more doors, but no sign of the bad guys.

Dust tickled her nose, and she wrinkled it to suppress a sneeze. She stood up and walked into the hall, and realized then the shooting outside had stopped. Her eyes wandered along the ceiling as she listened for footsteps on the roof. If anyone still moved around up there, she couldn't hear them.

The open door seemed as good a place to start as any. She winced as the floor creaked beneath her feet, and she kept the shotgun trained on the door. Motes of dust swirled in the sunlight, and she could see a patch of old, tacky carpeting and peeling wallpaper over a skirt of wainscoting through the gap.

Angie took a deep breath, then reached out with her left hand and pressed her fingertips to the door. The hinges groaned and she hopped back out of the doorway, anticipating a hail of bullets in response to the noise.

She leaned over, slow and easy, and peered around the doorjamb with one eye, then brought up the shotgun and swept it across the room. A living room, she decided, with a small kitchen and a short hallway on the right. Two windows on the opposite wall let in all the light.

A muffled thud sounded in the hallway behind her. She spun with the shotgun still pressed to her shoulder. A door handle rattled and hinges creaked. Footsteps approached from the down the hall to the left.

"Freeze," she said when the man reached the door.

He carried a hunting rifle in his right hand. He gasped, eyes wide. The rifle came up.

Angie shot him square in the chest, pumped, shot him again. Blood spattered the door and the frame as the man flew back and struck the far wall. He bounced off and fell forward, struck the doorjamb face first and rolled onto his side in the doorway. He didn't move, and his wide-eyed expression of shock went slack.

She kept the shotgun trained on the door. Did anyone follow him? Could someone have a gun trained on the door even now, waiting for her to show her face?

A shadow fell across the room.

Angie whirled and almost pulled the trigger when she saw the monstrous, lupine creature in the window. It snarled, baring its bloodied teeth as a pair of familiar brown eyes stared back at her.

An itch struck her trigger finger. The shotgun barrel lined up with the beast's face. One quick pull and she wouldn't have to worry about him when this was all over.

Then the beast was gone, climbing up toward the roof.

"Shit!"

Angie jumped over the body and into the hallway. He'd come from the left, and she saw one of the doors now hung open, swinging into the hall and toward her. She rushed over, swept the shotgun across the interior and found a utility or storage closet with metal shelves mounted to one wall and, just inside the door, a ladder climbing up to a hatch in the ceiling.

The shotgun would be too unwieldy in the hatchway. She set it against the wall and drew the .44. Its punch may come in handy, and the fewer of her own .40 caliber bullets investigators found, the fewer questions she had to answer.

She opened the .44's cylinder and plucked out the spent brass. She borrowed from one of the speedloaders to fill all five chambers, closed the cylinder, then climbed the ladder and waited on the top rung. As soon as the shooting started, she would pop up and cover Cole.

The first shot came three seconds later.

• • •

The shotgun blasts reverberated through the roof beneath Hess's feet.

"Goddamn it!" He turned his pistol on the hatch. "It's got to be the fed bitch!"

Denton moved out wide and trained his shotgun on the hatch.

Just show that pretty little head, Hess thought. One squeeze and they'd just have to worry about Tyler. With luck he'd be right behind her and they'd end it all right now.

Something moved out of the corner of his eye, something dark. He snapped his pistol around to see the wolfen Tyler climbing over the roof ledge.

Then Denton moved into his line of sight.

"Look out!" Hess shouted. He moved to his left to get a better shot.

Denton blasted away. Brick and mortar chips flew up from the roof ledge and Tyler dropped back over the side. Denton rushed toward the ledge.

The hatch popped open and the woman appeared. She held out a heavy revolver, drew a bead on Denton, took her shot.

Denton grunted and went down on his side. He dropped his shotgun.

Hess fired three rounds at her. One bullet punched through the hatch door just above her head. She ducked, then returned fire. He dodged to the right, put another bullet past her ear. She ducked down inside.

Denton groaned and rolled onto his back.

Hess shifted his aim back and forth from the roof ledge to the hatch and back again. Four shots left in this magazine. He had to make them count, or at least get a hold of Denton's weapon.

"Denton!" he called. "You okay?"

"She hit the vest," he said through gritted teeth. "But it may have gone through."

Sure enough, a red trickle flowed between his fingers as he held his right side.

"Give it up, sheriff!" the woman shouted. "It's over!"

Like hell.

She must think him an idiot if she expected him to answer. No way he'd give her an audible location. He took one more look toward the roof ledge, then took slow, quiet steps to his right to put the hatch door between them.

◆ ◆ ◆

Angie didn't expect Hess to give up so easy, but it was worth a shot. Now if Cole had another move, he'd best hurry up and make it. She couldn't hang from the ladder all day, and she hoped they hadn't tagged him.

The other cop writhed in pain. She could hear his labored breaths and occasional groans, and the skitch of his body or boots on the roof's rough surface. She only saw Hess and the other cop when she had popped her head up. With nobody else taking shots at her, she assumed they were the only ones on the roof.

Still no Cole. She couldn't wait any longer. She listened for any sign of Hess, anything at all.

A long grunt of pain from the deputy, then footsteps. Hess helping him to safety?

Angie took a tentative glance over the edge of the hatch's frame. The deputy half shuffled, half stumbled away, his back to her. No Hess.

The gunshot erupted to her left on the other side of the hatch. The hatch door, locked open on its hinges, flexed as something smacked against it. She ducked down and lost her footing on the ladder, and just managed to catch the top rung with the crook of her elbow before she could fall off.

Hess ran up behind her. She looked over her shoulder, stared straight into the barrel of his pistol.

This is it, she thought.

Something big and black slammed into Hess. He grunted hard as both went out of sight behind her.

Angie rushed up the ladder and banged her knee on the edge of the hatch as she tried to scramble onto the roof. The blow pitched her forward and she twisted as she fell, landing hard on her shoulder but holding the .44 out with both hands.

Hess shouted from beneath the wolf's massive form. The sheriff had his forearm jammed into the beast's mouth. Blood already soaked his sleeve. Angie drew a bead on Hess but couldn't get a clear shot.

A gunshot went off. The wolf jerked hard to one side and yelped like a kicked dog. Angie sat up and worked to get her feet under her, but the two kept fighting.

The wolf raked out one arm and Hess shouted again. His .45 flew out to one side and skittered across the roof, well out of reach. He struck the wolf in the legs and side with his knee and pounded its shoulders with the flat of his fist.

Angie got to her feet and glanced over at the fallen deputy. He was on his back, breathing in shallow gasps. Sweat covered his pale face and he stared up at the sky. No threat there.

Hess pulled his arm free and reached into the fur of the wolf's throat. The wolf's jaws darted down and clamped shut over Hess's face. Its mouth muffled his screams and he kicked and punched harder than ever.

◆ ◆ ◆

Blood.

Hess's blood. Cole relished it, so hot and sweet in his mouth.

The pain in his chest faded to a distant pinprick. Hess's blows fell on him like gentle rain. Cole felt his claws rend the sheriff's flesh. He heard the grind and scrape of his teeth on bone.

Hess screamed into Cole's throat. Cole felt him choke and gag on his own blood.

Cole bit and chomped and chewed. He swallowed a chunk of flesh. He chewed a bit of cartilage and went back for more. A cheekbone snapped and crushed between his teeth. His canines raked across bared skull.

Hess twitched beneath him. His arms went slack.

Cole shook his head, ripped loose another hunk of skin and muscle. Swallowed it. Savored it. He needed more. He needed to tear the sheriff open, needed to rip him apart. He needed—

To breathe.

Searing pain shot through his chest. His vision swam. He closed his eyes and a wave of dizziness fell over him. He struggled to draw a breath, struggled against the crushing weight in his chest.

He pushed himself up and away from Hess's body.

♦ ♦ ♦

Angie swept the revolver across the roof, scanned the rooftops across the street. No threats. She turned back to the beast and Hess.

Hess's kicking turned into rigid twitches that shuddered against the rooftop. His screams faded to gurgling gasps beneath the beast's jaws. Blood spread out in a glistening pool around his head.

At last Hess's body went slack. The beast released him, rocked back onto its haunches. The sheriff's ruined face slumped toward her, all red pulp and flayed flesh, one eye ruined or missing, the other lidless and smeared red, his nose just a stub and a black hole.

Angie gagged and looked away. She gagged again, took a deep breath to get it under control.

The beast stood up, slow, turned toward her. Blood dripped from its jaws. Its eyes fixed on hers.

Angie raised her weapon, aimed square at the beast's chest. Did it recognize her, or was she next?

The revolver trembled in her grip. Her finger tensed over the trigger.

THIRTY-SEVEN

NINA WENT DEEP INTO THE FOREST before undressing and triggering the change.

It had been a few years since she last walked on all fours, but she needed every advantage to find Sean and as a wolf she'd move faster and be able to pick up his scent easier. She felt he would head for home soon, and he'd have to come through this valley to get there.

She hoped she'd gotten ahead of him rather than fallen behind. If he panicked or otherwise lost it, it could be disastrous if he made it all the way back to the lodge.

The forest came alive around her. The scents, the sounds . . . she'd almost forgotten how much more vibrant the world seemed when she walked as a wolf. She put her nose to the ground and let the rich, heady aroma of the earth fill her nostrils. If she crossed her son's path, she would know it.

Nina made her way down into the valley. She stopped to sniff the air at regular intervals, and once caught a scent she dismissed as a black bear after a moment. The damp and decay of last season's leaves made it more difficult to pick out individual scents in spots, and before long she tracked her way up the opposite slope.

She worried again she'd missed him, that maybe he'd already crossed through, or passed through behind her. Or hell, maybe he took another route, or had no desire to go home. She shuddered to think of the damage he could cause running loose in town. Maybe she should double back and find her clothes and hightail it back to town and let Ronnie wait at the lodge.

Something rustled in the valley.

Nina perked up her ears and turned her head to face the sound. Whatever it was moved at a good clip as it trampled through the trees and brush. She crept back down on the slope, listening all the while for the intruder.

The noise passed along ahead of her. A large, dark shape lumbered through the trees.

Sean!

Nina circled around behind him. A tangle of scents fell across his trail, the strongest of which included the unmistakable tang of fresh blood.

She picked up speed and soon spotted him again. He traveled an awkward, zigzagging path down the valley, as if drunk or disoriented. Neither brush nor branches slowed him down, and if he couldn't just push past them he would knock them aside with a swipe of his claws.

Sean stopped as she approached. He growled and turned to face her, his arms held wide and claws spread.

Nina did not back down. The fur went up along her back, her tail stiffened, and she barked at him three times, short and sharp. His growl faltered, but he still snarled and did not lower his guard.

She darted forward, still snapping and barking. Sean shrunk away, cowed. He cringed as he relaxed his claws, then he turned and ran.

Nina sprinted after him. She closed the distance on his loping gait in the space of a hundred yards and zipped between his legs. His knee struck her shoulder and he tripped, tumbled to the ground and rolled alongside a tree. He shook off the confusion and started to rise, but Nina hopped onto his back and pressed him down.

She clamped her teeth down on the back of his neck, hard enough for it to hurt but not so hard to break skin. Sean whined and went down on his belly. The tension went out of his muscles.

After a moment Nina relaxed her grip a little, then a little more. Confident Sean would not fight back, she released him altogether and licked the fur behind his ear. The blood tasted sharp and strong, another taste she had not experienced in a long, long time.

She told herself she didn't miss it.

Sean closed his eyes. His breathing went deep and easy. Not asleep, but at least calm for the moment.

Nina settled down beside him and willed herself to change. Her shoulders rolled out and her hips tilted down. Her fingers and toes stretched back to their human proportions. In moments she lay nude beside her son. A shiver overcame her and goose pimples rose up along the length of her body.

She paid the cold no mind. She sat up and stroked Sean's neck and shoulder, gentle and loving. He rolled onto her lap and she pulled him in close to her bosom. Her arms encircled his large, lupine head.

"It's okay, baby," she whispered. "I'm here."

THIRTY-EIGHT

A LOW RUMBLE emerged from the beast's throat. It took a step toward Angie.

"Back down, Tyler!" Did he understand her? How much of him was still in there?

He took a second step, faltering this time, and pressed his right hand to his right side. Another low sound emerged from his throat.

Angie relaxed her grip. Tyler's eyes softened. The noise he made . . . a groan? Pain, not a threat. Tyler removed his hand from his side, and she saw the blood dripping from the tips of his fur on the right side of his chest. Blood bubbled up from the wound.

He kept coming. Angie stepped to one side and lowered the pistol. Tyler stumbled past her and toward the hatch. She watched as he lowered himself over it and dropped his legs into the opening.

"Tyler, wait!"

He disappeared below.

"Shit!" Angie crouched beside Hess's body and ignored the blood as she searched his pockets. A phone, but no keys. She stuffed the phone in her pocket as she looked around the roof. She almost missed the pile of keys beside one of the plumbing vents not thirty feet away.

Angie ran over to the keys. She tossed her rental keyring aside. The rest held various makes and models, two had black plastic key fobs. Different keychains held a photo of a young girl, a Miller-branded bottle opener, and a plastic cigar punch.

No time to debate. She grabbed a handful of keys and ran for the hatch.

"Help," a soft voice whispered.

The deputy lay flat on his back, his bloodied hands clenched to the hole in his vest. He craned his neck to look at her, his face pale and dotted with sweat.

Angie stepped up beside him. She looked up at the thick smoke blowing overhead. It wouldn't be long before the fires reached this street.

"Get me an ambulance," the deputy said.

Angie pointed the revolver at him.

"What, you're going to blow me away? Doesn't the Bureau frown on that shit?"

Angie pursed her lips. Two sides to every story, right? If this guy survived, Cole would be finished.

She pulled the trigger twice before she could have a second thought. The bullets slammed into the deputy's chest. At this range, his vest didn't stand a chance.

Angie tossed the .44 aside and went to the hatch. She stepped with care to avoid Tyler's blood streaking the edge and the ladder, and pulled the hatch closed as she descended.

A smear of blood marred the floor at the bottom. Had he fallen? A trail wound through the door, around the corner, and down the stairs. Angie raced down and out the front door.

She found Tyler lying on his stomach in the street. Most of his black fur had gone, replaced with a coarse tangle of dark hair. His head looked less lupine, his ears retracted and pulled down and his snout and jaws flattened into his face.

Angie dropped to her knees by his side. She ignored the asphalt scraping her knees as she reached under Tyler and rolled him onto his back. He grunted with the pain and his hands went to the wounds in his side.

She could see them both now: the entry wound just below his right breast and the exit wound several inches below his armpit. Bubbles erupted from the wounds with Tyler's every ragged breath.

Angie stripped off her shirt and stretched it across both wounds. Hess's bullet pierced Tyler's lung. If his lung collapsed he could go into shock or suffocate, if he didn't bleed out first. If she didn't get help soon, he'd be finished. She took Tyler's hands and pressed them to the wounds.

"Keep pressure on them! You hear me?"

Tyler nodded. She could feel his hands go tense, but there was little strength in them.

Angie ran to the cruiser near the back of the line of cars and started flipping through keys, ignoring anything that looked like a house key and jamming the rest into the trunk's lock one at a time.

Let him die. The thought struck hard, like a shout in her ear. It would be easy. Just jump in the car and drive away. Call an ambulance and leave the rest to fate.

No. She owed him. She knew now how he'd carried her away from the gunfight at the lodge, that he'd risked his own life to save hers then, and now. He trusted her with his secret.

Now she owed him to honor that trust.

A key on the third ring went in easy and popped the lock. She pocketed the set and dropped the rest on the street as she threw the trunk open. Among the various emergency tools and a gun case, she found a large red first aid kit. She pulled it out and ran back to Tyler's side.

"You still with me?"

He didn't respond, but his chest and belly still moved. The hair on his body receded even more, revealing his tanned skin. His face had returned to his familiar, human features, except for a protrusion around his mouth. It seemed to shrink more and more as she watched.

That had to be a good sign, she decided. She opened the first aid kit and pulled out the gauze and tape, then turned to Tyler. Her shirt peeled away from his flesh, freeing fresh rivulets of blood from the wounds. Blood plastered his side and pooled on the street. More air bubbled up to the surface.

Angie ripped open the gauze and slapped some over each wound. Blood helped paste the first layer to his skin and held it fast while she opened the tape. She used long strips of it to fasten the gauze in place and, she hoped, seal the wounds. Blood soaked the first gauze pad by the time she finished taping up the second.

She ran back to the cruiser, opened the door and popped the locks. She opened the back door wide, then returned to Tyler. He groaned and his eyes fluttered as she grabbed him beneath the shoulders and dragged him to the cruiser. His heels and legs scraped across the asphalt, but abrasions on his ass would be the least of his concerns if he survived this.

Her hip burned with the strain. She willed the still-healing muscle and tendons to hold together for just a few seconds longer. Her heart pounded and a brief dizzy spell struck her. Not now, she thought, and forced deep breaths in through her nose as she pulled. A bout of heat stroke would be the end for both of them.

Angie laid Tyler down and shoved his legs in line with the door, then backed in, reached down and grabbed his wrists. She braced her leg against the bottom of the door frame and pulled with all her might. Tyler's shoulders caught on the edge of the seat, then popped over. She tumbled back against the far door, but at least Tyler's upper half came with her. A long shove against his underarms and she finished the job.

His pulse beat slow and soft against the two fingers she pressed to his carotid. She squeezed back out of the car, shoved his legs inside, and slammed the door.

The bad guys didn't leave a lot of room between cars, but she didn't have much choice. The same key started the car. Angie shifted to drive, hammered the gas. The cruiser punched into the small, sporty pickup in front of it. She then popped the transmission into reverse, wrenched the wheel around and hit the gas again, backing into the larger pickup behind her.

Several more seconds of bumper cars and she managed to get free. The tires kicked up sand and dirt as she raced past the cars and whipped the car around in the intersection. Tyler bounced and shifted in the seat but offered no complaint as she raced out of Charity at top speed.

"You hang in there, Cole!" Angie shouted. "You hear me?"

This will be a fun one to explain: a suspended, beat-to-shit federal officer and a naked Indian, both covered in blood and riding in a stolen police cruiser.

She snatched up the radio mic. Whoever answered on the other side had best have an ER doc standing by, or they were going to be in at least as bad a shape as she and Tyler.

THIRTY-NINE

THE BACK DOOR TO UNCLE EVAN'S GARAGE was locked. Bobby smashed out a pane of glass with his elbow, then reached through and unlocked the door.

The old neon Budweiser sign hung over the small bar Evan set up at the back of the garage. Bobby lifted the sign off its hooks and set it behind the bar. The emergency phone rested on the electrical box mounted to the wall, still plugged into its tiny AC charger.

Bobby disconnected the phone and turned it on. The small screen flashed for a moment, then he had some signal bars and battery info. He found the button for the address book, found the single contact entry with the innocuous name "Home." Near as Bobby could tell, the number was far too long to be a regular phone number, but he selected it and pressed the green call button anyway.

The phone made a few clicks, then ringing started on the other side.

Another click, and the ringing stopped. Silence.

"Hello?" Bobby asked.

"Who's this?" A gruff voice. Firm.

"Bobby. Bobby Dunham. I'm, uh, a Sword."

"How did you get this phone?"

"My Uncle Evan is the chapter president, and, I . . . I think he's dead. Oh shit, I left him back there with that thing!" Bobby sniffled and wiped tears from his eyes as he spoke.

"Slow down, kid," the voice said, softer now. "What happened?"

"We were . . ." Bobby trailed off. He realized he didn't know who he was talking to. "We were taking care of club business. Then this fuckin' . . . monster thing came out and started tearing guys apart! It looked like some kind of movie werewolf!"

Silence on the other end.

"Are you there?" Bobby asked. "Hello?"

"Please hold."

"Hold? What the fuck, man? I—hello? Hello!?"

Bobby kicked the dining room chair over. How the hell could they put him on hold? He just told them Uncle Evan, a club president, could be dead!

Bobby paced the room for the next minute, stopping only to peer out the front and side blinds from time to time. He wondered if he shouldn't just hang up and head back for Chicago when someone finally picked up on the other side.

"Bobby." A new voice, this one deeper, softer.

"About time, man! Who the fuck are you people? I can't keep waiting around!"

"I'm here to help you, Bobby. Where are the others?"

"Uh-uh, man. I ain't saying shit until I know who you are."

"I'm the man who sent you to Minnesota, Bobby. The man who sends you your meth. The man who brews up the special additive that gives it that special kick."

Bobby suddenly felt lightheaded. "Oh, shit, the drugs! Sir, I'm sorry, we had an incident at the Hammer, and some cops showed up and shoved us around. They didn't find the drugs, though, we had them hidden real good, and then we took them—"

"Fuck the drugs."

"What?"

"The drugs are meaningless, son. Tell me more about this 'monster' you saw."

◆ ◆ ◆

The Minnesota project bore fruit much sooner than Winfield had anticipated.

He jotted several notes while Bobby told his story, and asked few questions. He directed Bobby to leave his bike and his colors behind and get to the airport. Then he hung up and made several more brief calls.

In just a few hours, Bobby Dunham would disappear and Winfield would be closer to some real answers.

There was still much to be done. Much to prepare for.

Winfield took off his lab coat and tossed it across the back of his chair. He ripped his notes off the notebook, folded them up, and stuffed them in his front pants pocket. Then he turned off his desk lamp and went out into the lab. He directed his assistants to clean up as he walked out the door.

As he waited for the elevator at the end of the hall, he pulled an encrypted cell phone out of his pocket, one similar to the phone Bobby used. He dialed a number from memory.

The phone rang four times on the other end. The nurse picked up.

"Hello?"

"Put him on," Winfield said.

The phone clattered as she set it down for a moment. Winfield could hear muffled voices on the other end, then someone picked up the phone again.

"Silas? This better be important." The old man's voice sounded as dry and brittle as his weathered old body.

"Oh, it is," Winfield said. "We found them."

FORTY

NINA GRIPPED THE STEERING WHEEL a little harder as she turned onto the lodge driveway and made the climb to the lodge proper. She expected police tape and flashing red and blue lights, but the office and lodge building sat dark and quiet. A few visitors' cars were parked out front, but she saw no sign of movement. She breathed a sigh of relief and drove down their private drive and to the house.

Sean lay curled in the Wrangler's narrow back seat, wearing only his jeans and Nina's coat. He didn't come around enough to speak until well after nightfall, and even then he could only say someone attacked the gym and injected him with some kind of drug. With her fur pushed back out for warmth, she waited a few more hours before finding her clothes again and leading him out of the valley.

Nina parked the Wrangler behind the house, then climbed out and popped the driver's seat forward. She reached inside and gave Sean a gentle shake on his shoulder.

"Wake up, honey. We're home."

Sean sat up and looked around. He allowed Nina to help him out of the Jeep and held her jacket tight around his shoulders as he walked through the cold, damp grass.

Ronnie opened the back door as they reached the stoop.

"Sean! What happened?"

"Leave him be," Nina said.

Ronnie made way as she led Sean into the house.

"Where have you guys been? Are you alright, Sean?"

"He's not feeling well. Let him get some sleep and we'll figure it out in the morning."

"But Ma, it's almost midnight! I—"

Nina stopped in the living room and whirled around to face Ronnie. "I. Said. Wait."

Sean stopped beside her. He stood in a daze, bathed in the soft light of the table lamp and the cool glow of the television set. On screen, a frozen image of a vaguely familiar action star fired a machine gun and shouted into the camera. Sean blinked and stared at nothing.

Ronnie threw up his hands and walked away.

Nina led Sean to his bedroom. She took the jacket from him and guided him to the bed. He crawled in and rolled toward the wall, his back to her. Nina laid a hand on his shoulder, squeezed.

"You rest up, baby. Everything's okay now." She pulled his sheet and blanket up to his chest and closed the bedroom door on her way back to the living room.

Ronnie stood near the television. He shut it off and turned to face her.

"Well?"

"Have we heard from Cole yet?" She kept walking as she spoke.

"Not yet." Ronnie followed her into the kitchen. "So what happened?"

"The bikers attacked them at the gym. They shot him up with some kind of drug." Nina opened the fridge and pulled out containers of leftovers. Chicken, chili, the deli-cut roast beef. Anything with protein. She didn't want to deal with Ronnie now, she needed to replenish.

"The bikers from the wood shop? What the hell for? What kind of drug?"

"I don't know, Ronnie! I told you, he's not feeling well. He's barely coherent. Let him rest and we'll figure it out."

"Fine, fine. It's just . . . shit."

"I know." She scooped some cold chicken into her mouth before tossing the bowl into the microwave. She punched a few buttons and hit start.

Ronnie leaned against the counter. She enjoyed the silence as she rolled up a slice of roast beef and ate it. It couldn't last, though. She had too many questions of her own.

"What did you and Sean talk about last night?"

"When?"

"He said you spoke down in the hollow. I know you were drunk, Ronnie, but I need to know what you told him."

He pushed off of the counter. "What are you saying, Ma? That this is my fault somehow?"

"All I'm saying is he was all fired up to go to the gym today, and I want to know why. Why now, of all times? Something must have set him off!"

"Unfucking real, Ma. You cut me out of everything Cole's got going on, and when Sean runs into trouble, somehow that's my fault!"

"That's not what I said."

"You didn't have to! It's pretty clear where I stand in this family!"

He stormed out of the kitchen.

Nina's shoulders sagged. She put down her food and went into the living room. Ronnie grabbed his jacket off the couch and put it on as he walked to the door.

"Where are you going?" she asked.

"Away. I'm grabbing some stuff and taking the Ram. Call me when you know what's up with Cole. I might answer."

"What? Ronnie, you can't leave!"

He stopped in the door and gave her an irritated look, then shook his head and walked out the door. She rushed through the living room and out onto the porch.

"Ronnie, stop! Come on, we need you! I need you!"

"Funny, you've gotten along just fine without me until now." He didn't even break stride as he walked across the yard.

"Don't do this, Ronnie," she called. "Ronnie!"

Cold shoulder. Well done, Nina, she thought. She closed the front door and went back to the kitchen. The microwave beeped. She punched the door button and pulled out her chicken. Tendrils of steam rose up as she tossed the meat with her fork.

Two days. She lost all four of her children in two short days. Oh, what John must think of her now.

Nina hurled the chicken dish into the sink as hard as she could and screamed. Tears came next, hot and heavy. She sat down hard at the kitchen table and wept into her hands.

FORTY-ONE

COLE'S HEART MONITOR emitted a soft beep at regular intervals. Angie didn't even notice it anymore. She sat beside his bed, flipping through a novel she picked up in the hotel gift shop. Her eyes followed the words on the page, but her mind wandered.

The doctors moved him out of intensive care three days ago. His vitals looked good and the surgery went well. Unfortunately, they couldn't tell her why he had yet to wake up long enough to utter more than a few incoherent sentences.

Angie tossed the book on the floor. She felt like she should be in the field, but she didn't dare leave his side, even if the Bureau hadn't turned her leave of absence into a suspension.

Pending investigation, of course.

She reached over and rested a hand on top of Cole's. When he woke up, they had a lot to sort out.

• • •

Nina needed a break. She locked up the office, hung the "closed" sign, and walked to the house. If the lodge visitors wanted something, they would just have to wait. They should consider themselves lucky she didn't cancel all reservations for the week. With Cole hospitalized, Ronnie gone and Amy quitting the day after, it left the lodge very short-handed.

She should be in Nevada with Cole, but Sean needed her, too. This morning, he forgot about guiding a Tennessee Boy Scout troop on their hike. Two days ago, he almost rolled his Wrangler while taking a supposed shortcut between trails. Last week, he threatened to break a customer's nose in an argument over a discarded soda can.

The living room light shone through the windows. Nina went inside and found the kitchen light had been left on, too. She turned them both off and went down the hall to Sean's room. Light leaked out from beneath the door and she could hear soft music on the other side.

Nina knocked on the door. No answer, so she knocked again.

"Sean? Is everything alright?" She opened the door.

Sean lay on his bed with one arm propped under his pillow. He stared up at the ceiling.

"Talk to me, Sean. I'm here to help."

He rolled onto his side and faced the wall.

Tears welled up in Nina's eyes. What more could she say? She walked out and closed the door behind her.

◆ ◆ ◆

Diana's phone vibrated against her thigh. She leaned back in her chair and pulled it out, read the display. Mom. Diana hit the power button to kill the ringer and tossed the phone onto the table beside her coffee. She dove back into her biochem notes before noting the flashing LED on her phone.

"Damn it." She dropped her pencil and picked up the phone. The voice mail icon lit up on the display. Diana called in and punched in her passcode.

"I need you to call me, Diana. There's a lot going on. Just . . . come home, okay? Our family is falling apart."

"Fat chance." Diana deleted the message.

◆ ◆ ◆

Winfield picked up the phone and dialed a number from memory. A gruff voice picked up on the other side.

"Ops."

"It's me. Get your team together. You're going to college."

◆ ◆ ◆

Ronnie pulled up to Amy's small house and saw her little blue Civic in the driveway. What the hell was she still doing home? She said she would be working at the gym until late tonight.

He parked at the curb and went inside. No sign of Amy in the dim living room or kitchen. Something beeped in the living room. He turned on the light and found Amy's cell phone on the floor between the couch and the TV tray she used for her laptop. It beeped again, notifying her of two missed calls, a voice mail, and a few text messages.

He set the phone on the tray. Maybe she stayed home because she didn't feel well. The gym should have notified her clients, though. They didn't need to be harassing her on her cell.

Then he saw the cane. An elegant thing, made of a dark, knotted wood with a sturdy perpendicular handle. It leaned against the wall near the hallway. Ronnie moved around the couch and reached out for it, saw the jacket on the floor.

A black men's suit jacket, lying in a heap just a few feet into the hall. Beyond it, a few steps closer to the bedroom door, laid a thin, black necktie, still tied in a loop.

Ronnie's hands tightened into fists. A client? Some other beau she'd been hiding from him? He stepped over the discarded clothing and listened at the bedroom door.

Silence.

They had to be in there, maybe curled up and napping on the bed, having lost track of time. He opened the door slow. Quiet. He didn't want to give the guy any warning before beating the living shit out of him.

Everything in the room was red. Ronnie's breath caught in his throat. Blood. On the walls, on the floor, sprayed across the mirror mounted to the dresser.

Ronnie threw the door wide open. Amy lay on the bed, naked and spread-eagle. Blood soaked the tangled bedsheets and fanned across the headboard and wall. Her abdomen had been torn open, her guts spread across the bed. Bites marred her neck and breasts, and a row of four deep gouges ran down her right thigh. Her jaw hung slack, her half-lidded eyes stared at the ceiling.

An old man clung to the headboard to support his hunched, frail body. He stood naked, covered with blood from his sunken chest to his withered penis. Blood pasted his long, white hair to his shoulders. Bits of gore covered his hands and clung to his lips, chin and cheeks.

The old man grinned, showing off long, red-stained teeth.

"Hello, grandson."

AFTERWORD

It's all about family.

Whether we're talking motorcycle clubs or wolf packs, the members of a family have to function as a unit. When things are going well, a family is at peace. When there's trouble and turmoil, a family has to pull together or it all comes apart.

The Swords know how it works. These guys are brothers, and they depend on one another. When the shit hit the fan, they rallied behind their president, Evan. It may not have worked out for them in the end, but they stuck together and acted as a unit.

It's a different story for the Tyler family. A series of disasters has left them divided, starting with the death of their patriarch. Without an alpha, the two eldest brothers jockey for position. Then one of their youngest is murdered, and guilt and blame burn hot between them. Grief is a powerful thing, especially for an introverted and secretive family like the Tylers. Then baby sister bails and tension is at an all-time high.

Enter Angie Wallace. Woof! Tell me you've never seen a family torn apart by a woman coming into the picture, driving wedges between mothers and sons or dividing siblings. To top it off, there's not a family on this Earth that likes a stranger digging into their dirty little secrets—worse still, when it's the government doing the digging.

Angie certainly hasn't done the family any favors. One brother gone, another on the verge of death, and a whole new set of bodies in her wake. When Angie learned John Tyler had changed his name, she wondered what he was trying to hide. If she hadn't been blinded by her pursuit of the truth behind Cole and his family, she might have stopped to wonder what John Tyler might have been hiding *from*. Will Angie be the *coup de grace* for the Tyler family?

I guess that would be telling.

The great thing about a family like the Tylers is they bring me a wealth of material. Not just in the characters themselves and their relationships to one another, but also in their histories. The family members each have their own pasts and futures, and their actions have had an influence on the people around them. Not only have they told me what's next, they've told me what's gone down before, back to previous generations. I'll be sharing most of it as the novel series continues, but there will be more short stories like "Bravo Four." We'll have a few other surprises for you as well.

I'm not done with the Swords, either. Not by a long shot. Evan and company may have ridden their last ride, but who sent them to Minnesota, and why? What are they mixing into their drugs? Like the Tyler family, the Lucifer's Swords MC has its own long and sordid past and its own stories to tell. You will get to know them better soon.

If *Lie with the Dead* is your first exposure to *The Pack*, welcome to the family! I hope you enjoyed it. To those of you returning after *Winter Kill*, I thank you, and I hope it was worth the wait. Reader response to that book continues to blow me away, from both horror and crime fans alike. And if you've been following along since *Werewolves: Call of the Wild*? Goddamn. I'm not sure what to say other than you're amazing.

I assure you, we're just getting warmed up.

Mike Oliveri
Peoria
June 2013

ABOUT THE AUTHOR

Mike Oliveri won a Bram Stoker Award for his first novel, *Deadliest of the Species*, which has since been reprinted by Evileye Books. He has written several short stories, novellas, and comics in the horror and thriller genres.

Mike is a displaced Chicago suburbanite who calls Peoria, Illinois home. He doesn't miss the Chicago traffic, but nobody in Peoria knows how to make a proper Italian beef sandwich or Chicago-style pizza. He is a martial artist, family man, motorcyclist, and cigar aficionado, but not necessarily in that order.

Readers can learn more about Mike and his work on the Web at MikeOliveri.com or catch him on Twitter:

@MikeOliveri.

ABOUT EVILEYE BOOKS

Evileye Books publishes horror, crime, supernatural thrillers, and science fiction. For more information please visit our website at Evileyebooks.com.

If you share our love of stories that consume you, consider some of our titles out now:

Bone Welder
By Ray Bradbury Award winner Greg Kishbaugh

DarkWalker
by John Urbancik

Creeping Stones
By New York Times best-selling author Cullen Bunn

Never Bet the Devil & Other Warnings
By Orrin Grey

The Dead Sheriff: Zombie Damnation
By Mark Justice

The Burning Maiden Anthology
Edited by Greg Kishbaugh

Featuring award winning
best-selling authors

Joe R. Lansdale

Matthew Pearl

Charles Johnson

Lyndsay Faye

Louis Bayard

Mort Castle

Sarah Langan

Bruce Boston

Cullen Bunn

Steven Barnes

www.ingramcontent.com/pod-product-compliance
Lightning Source LLC
Chambersburg PA
CBHW020743250626
47155CB00003B/896